Ashley thinks Dar is divine

Ashley snapped up the phone. "Hello?"

"This is Dar Barrington. Is Ashley there?"

She couldn't breathe. Her hands trembled. "This is Ashley," she replied.

"Hi, I'm glad I caught you. We're going to rehearse for the dance at the middle school tomorrow. I was wondering if you want to come hear us."

Ashley's heart banged in her chest. Was this an official-business kind of call, or was it something more personal? "Sounds good. Should I call Rachel and ask her to join us?" she asked.

"No, don't call her," Dar replied. "The truth is, I just really want to see you again."

Ashley's
Love Angel

FOREVER ANGELS

Ashley's Love Angel

Suzanne Weyn

Text copyright © 1997 by Chardiet Unlimited, Inc., and Suzanne Weyn.
Cover illustration copyright © 1997 by Mark English.
Cover border photography by Katrina.
Angel stickers (GS17) copyright © 1991 by Gallery Graphics, Inc., Noel, MO 64854. Used with permission.

Published by Troll Communications L.L.C.

Printed in the United States of America.

10   9   8   7   6   5   4   3   2   1

For Carolan Weyn, a spunky angel

Ashley's Love Angel

1

Ashley looked up sharply, pulled abruptly from her pleasant daydream by the squeal of turning tires. Her brother Jeremy spun the steering wheel frantically as he jammed on the brakes, sending the car sliding sideways down the twisting country road.

Instinctively, Ashley dropped down in her seat behind Jeremy. With one hand she sheltered her head. With the other, she clutched the arm of her friend Christina, who sat beside her in the backseat, rigid with surprise and fear.

The car bounced off a tree and careened to one side, its back end swinging to the right while the front end went left. Hard-pressed brakes sent up a shrill, high-pitched whine of complaint.

The car slid, then spun in a dizzying circle. Wincing with terrified anticipation, Ashley knew it was only a matter of seconds before they crashed into something. Crashed hard.

Her eyes tightly closed, she braced for the awful impact. "Get down!" she shouted to Christina, who sat forward in her seat, her eyes glued to something in the road.

Christina didn't seem to hear her. She remained sitting up, oddly entranced. In shock, too scared to move, Ashley decided.

Desperate, she grabbed Christina's arm, yanking her to the side. "I said get down!"

The car spun again. Then stopped.

There was no crash. No sound of crunching metal. No neck-wrenching jolt.

Her heart racing, Ashley dared to open her eyes. "What happened?" she asked, her quavering voice small and tight. She reached out and touched her brother's arm. "Are you okay?"

Jeremy nodded as he sat, ghostly pale, wide-eyed, his back plastered against the seat, his white-knuckled hands still clutching the steering wheel. He breathed heavily, obviously very shaken. "Oh, wow!" he muttered. "Wow!"

"What?" Ashley demanded, her voice growing stronger. There didn't seem to be anything in the road, no other car. Nothing. "Did you slide on an ice patch back there?"

Then she saw him.

On the side of the winding country road stood a dark-haired boy, clutching his bike as though he were using it to keep his knees from buckling. Behind him, thick-trunked pine trees seemed to shiver in the piercing winter wind.

Ashley decided he was about the same age as she and Christina, thirteen. But she'd never seen him before. That was odd. Everyone in the small, rural town of Pine Ridge knew one another, especially kids around the same age. Most of them had gone to school together since kindergarten.

The boy stooped to search for something. His hand glided over the smooth black frames of a pair of eyeglasses. The boy picked them up and repositioned them on his broad nose. The right lens had cracked down the middle.

"The buck almost creamed my car, but it saved that kid's life," Jeremy choked out. "He just darted out of the woods on his bike. If I hadn't braked for the deer I would have hit him for sure."

"What buck?" Ashley asked.

"The big deer that ran into the road," Jeremy said as the color slowly returned to his face. "He bolted out of the trees, stopped in the middle of the road, ran off in the other direction. Didn't you see him?"

"I closed my eyes and ducked," Ashley admitted sheepishly.

Shutting off the engine, Jeremy got out of the car. "Are you all right?" he called as he strode quickly to the boy on the bike.

The boy nodded. Sitting in the backseat, Ashley couldn't hear the conversation they were having, but the kid did seem to be okay. Just shaken.

Ashley studied the boy through the window. He was a geeky sort of kid. His jeans were just a bit too short, revealing an expanse of white sock over scuffed loafers. The frames of his battered glasses were taped on one side. He shrunk away from Jeremy as if afraid Jeremy might yell at him.

Ashley turned to Christina, at her side. The spinning of the car had tossed Christina's long, wavy, wheat-colored hair into her face, but she hardly seemed aware of it. Her round sky-blue eyes seemed to be focusing on some faraway place.

Ashley gently jiggled her friend's arm. "Are you okay?" she inquired softly. "Christina? Hey!"

Roused from her trance, Christina blinked and turned to Ashley. She looked oddly happy, her pretty face beaming with an inner light.

"Are you okay?" Ashley repeated the question.

Christina nodded absently.

"Have you ever seen that kid before?" Ashley asked, pointing to the boy beside Jeremy. "I wonder why he's riding a bike in this weather?"

Christina shook her head. "It wasn't a buck at all," she said softly, half to herself.

"Huh?" Ashley said, raking her mane of curly red hair in confusion. "What? Are you talking about the animal Jeremy saw? Do you mean it was a doe? It's kind of hard to tell the difference in winter when the bucks have shed their antlers."

"It wasn't a deer at all," Christina clarified. "It wasn't even an animal."

Ashley furrowed her delicate brows into a questioning expression. "What are you talking about?"

Christina leaned closer, her voice an awed whisper. "It was an angel. An angel stepped in front of the car and saved that boy."

"An angel?" Ashley echoed. That certainly explained Christina's dazed, amazed expression. She'd just seen an angel. But Jeremy said a deer jumped in front of his car. Even Ashley knew that a deer didn't look anything like an angel. "Are you sure?" she questioned.

"Positive," Christina said, nodding. "A gorgeous, shining, huge angel. Almost nine feet tall, I'd guess. He had gigantic golden wings and long golden hair—but it was more like sunbeams instead of hair. He had the most beautiful lavender-blue eyes. He appeared in the road just as that boy came out of the woods. Then the angel pushed the front of the car to the side. He just barely touched it."

Ashley turned sharply to look at the boy, who was still speaking to Jeremy on the side of the road. "If the angel saved his life, why did Jeremy say that he saw a deer?"

"I don't know," Christina said, thinking about this. "It seems as though everyone doesn't see angels the way we do."

"I wonder why that is?" Ashley considered this as she sat back in her seat. Why did she and her friends Christina, Katie, and Molly see angels now? Was it because they'd discovered the bridge in the woods? Ashley thought for a minute. Yes, she was sure the bridge must hold the answer.

The Angels Crossing Bridge was a dilapidated covered

bridge hidden deep in the Pine Manor Woods, which stood beside the horse ranch Ashley's parents owned. The bridge was where she and her friends had first encountered three eccentric angels named Ned, Norma, and Edwina.

Ever since that first meeting, angels seemed to surround the girls. Or were they now simply aware of the angels that had been there all along? Ashley couldn't be sure.

Her thoughts were interrupted as Jeremy opened the car door and swung back into the driver's seat. "What a weird kid," he declared as he shut the door. "I offered him a ride, but he said he didn't want one. Wouldn't tell me where he was going. I asked him why he rode out of the woods without looking. He said he had things on his mind."

"What's his name?" Ashley asked.

"Jason Hudson."

Ashley watched as the boy took off down the road, pedaling away with determination, his head down, bent on getting wherever he was going. She wondered if he had any idea how lucky—how *blessed*—he was? Did he see the angel in the road? Probably not, Ashley decided.

"Well, we might as well get to the high school so you can hear that band," Jeremy said, turning on the car once again.

"Might as well," Ashley agreed. "I hope they're better than the bands I've been hearing. They've all been awful."

Jeremy eased the car onto the right side of the road and they continued on. As they passed the biking boy, Ashley peered out at him, curious. With his head down, he didn't even notice the passing car.

Who *was* he? Why hadn't she ever seen him before? And what had he been doing near the woods? Certainly not riding his bike. The ground was way too rocky and uneven for that to be any fun.

The distance between them widened, and Ashley thought about angels once again. She wished she'd seen this one. Although her awareness of angels was greatly heightened, actually seeing one was still thrilling.

They were beautiful beyond description. With every sighting, Ashley felt somehow stronger, more at one with herself and the entire world. Just to see one was a gift to be treasured. And Ashley and her friends had seen so many.

She even talked to them. At first she was so awestruck she could barely put two words together. But as Ashley got to know the kind and gentle angels, she became more comfortable around them. Now she could speak easily with them.

Christina had settled back into her seat wearing a blissful expression. She was probably still seeing the angel in her mind's eye.

Shutting her eyes, Ashley tried to imagine how the angel must have looked. She remembered Christina's description of him, and she pictured the giant angel pushing aside the car with one effortless gesture. Her mind filled so completely with the image that it was almost as if she had seen it with her own eyes. An incredibly peaceful feeling swept over her as Jeremy drove on to the high school.

2

Jeremy turned into the parking lot of Pine Ridge High School. "Thanks for the ride," Ashley said as she and Christina climbed out of the car. "Can you pick us up in an hour?"

"Sure. Meet me back here," Jeremy said, putting the car in gear. He drove away as Ashley and Christina climbed the stone steps to the high school's massive front door.

As the girls entered the school lobby, the shrill whine of a microphone being turned on immediately told them where to find the band they had come to hear. Human Dilemma was obviously practicing in the cafeteria down the main corridor. "Is Rachel going to be here, too?" Christina asked.

"Yes," Ashley said with a laugh. "My co-chairperson, the happiest girl on earth, will be here, too."

Christina shoved Ashley lightly. "Don't be mean. Rachel is great."

"I know, but she's so *happy*. I never met anyone so optimistic in my life."

"I'm optimistic," Christina countered.

"Yeah, but not like Rachel. No one is as optimistic as Rachel. She's off the optimism charts. I don't think that girl has ever had a bad day."

Rachel Rodriguez had been elected, along with Ashley, as chairperson for the upcoming eighth-grade winter dance. Their first big challenge was to find a good band. Although the girls had already listened to several bands made up of kids from the middle school, none had satisfied them.

"I bet Rachel's a Sagittarius," Christina surmised thoughtfully. As usual, she assumed Rachel's boundless optimism, like most things, could be explained by looking to the stars. Horoscope, tarot readings, palmistry, numerology—these things supplied Christina with all the answers she needed. Most of the time, anyway. "Sagittarians tend to be very upbeat and they send out lots of positive energy," she considered. "I'm going to ask her if she just had a birthday this past December."

The girls stepped into the cafeteria and were immediately assaulted by the blare of staticky reverberations from the band's speakers.

Ashley spotted slim, petite Rachel standing to the left of the band, her long, shiny black hair pulled off her delicate face in a streaming ponytail. Rachel saw Ashley, and waved, flashing a megawatt smile of sparkling white teeth.

The girls joined Rachel, who, as always, bubbled with enthusiasm. "This band is definitely it," she declared excitedly. "They have just what we've been looking for."

"Have you heard them already?" Ashley asked eagerly.

"No, but I can just tell. Look at them." She nodded toward the four band members, who were huddled in a corner tuning up their musical equipment. "They're adorable."

The boys were, indeed, all good-looking, each in a different way, but the one tall boy who stood at the center of the group was especially movie-star handsome. His dark brown hair was shaggy, reaching almost to his broad shoulders. Large, expressive brown eyes beamed out from his squarish face. Ashley couldn't stop staring at him.

Rachel followed Ashley's gaze and laughed lightly. "That's Dar Barrington you're staring at. He's the lead singer and songwriter. My sister's a freshman here, and she told me that all the girls totally love him. He's a junior, I think."

"What's he like?" Ashley asked as she studied the curve of his face.

"I don't know," Rachel admitted, "but I bet he's very nice. Otherwise everyone wouldn't like him so much. Would they?"

"Rachel, were you born in early December?" Christina broke in.

"How did you know?" Rachel cried. "Wow! You're a genius! Are you psychic?"

"No, you just seem like a Sagittarian. Happy, upbeat, you know," Christina replied matter-of-factly.

Rachel's brows furrowed. "Sagittarians can also be too blunt, even tactless."

"I've never heard you be tactless," Ashley said honestly.

Rachel rolled her dark eyes. "Believe me, I've put my foot in my mouth more than once." Her expression lightened and she shrugged. "Oh, well, nobody's perfect, I guess."

Dar Barrington stepped up to his microphone. He spoke directly to the girls. "Hi, ladies. Thanks for letting us audition for your dance. We hope you dig what you hear. This first song was written by our drummer, Ricky, and myself." He turned to his band and gave them the beat. "One, two, three . . ."

The band launched into a hard-driving rock number. Rachel smiled at Christina and Ashley. "See? I knew it. Seriously rockin'."

Ashley nodded and flashed a thumbs-up sign. She had to agree. Human Dilemma had a great sound. And they were really professional. Not at all like the tinny, off-key middle school bands the girls had been hearing. She started moving with the beat. This band would definitely get the kids dancing.

Human Dilemma did five more songs, three originals and two by other groups. As she listened, Ashley found her attention totally focused on Dar. Wow, he was gorgeous. But it was more than that. He had so much stage presence that he seemed to be commanding Ashley to look at him. His eyes flashed with powerful emotions as he sang.

Dar must be so interesting to talk to, Ashley thought as she listened to the words he'd written. Sensitive, smart—not like the boys she knew at Pine Ridge Middle School. A sudden hunger to know Dar Barrington better grew inside her.

When the fifth song ended, the girls clapped and cheered. The band members bowed and smiled appreciatively. Dar sauntered over to the three of them, pushing his hair from his handsome face. "Well?" he asked. "What did you think?"

"Awesome!" Rachel answered without hesitating.

Ashley was glad Rachel had leaped in to answer the question. Being so close to Dar made her unexpectedly nervous. She clasped her hands together tightly to keep them from trembling.

"How long has the band been together?" Christina inquired enthusiastically.

"Since eighth grade," Dar replied. He continued explaining how the band had formed and told about some of their bigger gigs. They'd played at a bunch of private parties, even done a small wedding. But all the while Dar spoke to the group, his light brown eyes were fixed on Ashley.

She felt caught between shyness and flattery. Part of her wanted to hide, his gaze unnerved her so much. But the other part was thrilled he seemed interested in her. "What did *you* think of the band?" he finally asked, speaking very directly to Ashley.

"Oh . . . um . . . you were great. I'd say you've got the job." She looked to Rachel for confirmation on this, and Rachel nodded emphatically. "If you want it, that is."

"Sure we do," he agreed. He flashed Ashley the warmest smile she'd ever seen. "Thanks."

They discussed the details—where, when, how much the committee could pay the band. Dar's interest in Ashley slowly became apparent to Rachel and Christina. At one point, Christina caught Ashley's eye and smiled. Ashley looked away quickly, afraid Dar would catch the secret exchange between them and figure out they were thinking about him.

"I'd better take your phone number," Dar said to Ashley.

"What?" she murmured, too surprised to believe her ears.

"In case I need to discuss anything with you—about the dance," he explained.

"Oh, of course, sure," Ashley said in one gush of air. "Sure. I'll give you mine. You'd better take Rachel's number, too. You can call her if you can't get in touch with me."

Rachel wrote her phone number on a pad, then handed it to Ashley. "Thanks. I'll be in touch," Dar said as he slipped the piece of paper in his pocket and left to rejoin his band.

"I don't think he'll be calling *me*," Rachel giggled.

The hot burn of an embarrassed blush swept across Ashley's face.

"He really likes you." Christina gleefully stated the obvious.

"Do you think so?" Ashley asked anxiously. Though she knew he seemed to like her, she wanted to hear someone else confirm her suspicion so that it would be absolutely real.

Right now it didn't seem possible. He was a junior, practically a local rock star. All the high school girls were crazy about him. Why should he be interested in her?

"Sure he likes you," Christina insisted. "Couldn't you tell?"

"He was probably being extra nice to me to make sure they got the job," Ashley said. She wanted to be logical, not to set herself up with false hopes.

Rachel shook her head. "I don't think so. I'm a chairperson, too. He didn't stare at me the whole time," she pointed out.

Ashley had to admit this was true. Both Christina and Rachel were really pretty, too. Christina, so long-legged and blond with those startling blue eyes. And Rachel was like a perfect doll. Her features so delicate; her hair so long, black, and silky; and her dark eyes rimmed with heavy black lashes.

It wasn't as if Dar had focused his attention on Ashley because the other girls were homely or dull. They weren't.

For some reason, he must have really liked her. "He's probably just a flirty kind of guy," Ashley said. She still couldn't believe there was anything in her that would attract an amazing guy like Dar.

"He didn't flirt with us," Christina reminded her.

"I suppose," Ashley had to admit. "Well, I won't ever see him again, so what does it matter?"

"You'll see him at the dance," Rachel said.

Ashley sighed. "Yeah, but not . . . you know . . . we won't be alone."

"You never know," Christina insisted mischievously. "Come over to my place later. I'll do a tarot card reading. We'll see what your future holds."

3

"Love is everywhere," Christina sang, dancing around Ashley as they walked down the hall of Pine Ridge Middle School the next morning.

She'd been singing it ever since she did Ashley's tarot reading the night before.

"Would you cut it out," Ashley demanded, laughing despite herself. Christina was being goofy, but Ashley really didn't mind.

"You saw the cards," Christina said knowingly, stopping at her locker and turning the combination. "They were chock-full of romance. You were *surrounded* by love cards."

Ashley kept an open mind about Christina's beliefs, but she didn't share her friend's complete faith in the tarot or any of that sort of stuff. It might be true—it might not be. She changed her mind constantly. Christina told her this kind of uncertainty was perfectly natural, since she was born under the sign of Libra, represented by weighing scales. Libra was always balancing everything.

The tarot card reading had been encouraging, though. A card showing an approaching prince came up right next to the center card, which represented Ashley. Was Dar Barrington her prince? He sure seemed like one onstage. He was so confident and at ease as he sang. And so good-looking.

A tall girl with an energetic, athletic walk and bouncy, shoulder-length auburn hair came toward them. Her baseball cap was turned brim backward. "Hey, guys," Katie Nelson said, leaning against the locker beside Christina's. "How was that band yesterday? Could they actually carry a tune? Can they play modern music?"

"They were amazing," Christina informed her.

"Yeah?" Katie inquired, her amber eyes widening with interest. "Tell."

Christina told more about Dar Barrington's flirtation with Ashley than about the band itself. "Cool," Katie commented. "Hey, I should break this story in next week's *Writer*," she teased. Katie regularly wrote and took photos for the school paper. "I can see the headline now: Dance Chairperson and Rock Star in Cosmic Love Connection!"

"Don't you dare!" Ashley cried, too aghast at the idea to realize that Katie was kidding.

"What's going on?" Molly Morgan joined the group. Today she'd twisted her white-blond hair into thick braids and wrapped them around her head.

"What's with the Heidi look?" Katie asked in her usual blunt fashion.

Ashley smiled sheepishly because Molly did look a bit like Heidi. In addition to the braids, Molly wore a balloon-sleeved white peasant blouse under a black velvet vest embroidered with a Tyrolean flower design. Black velvet leggings and ankle-high black boots completed the outfit.

If Katie hadn't drawn the Heidi comparison, Ashley would have liked the outfit. She and Molly shared a love of style and nice clothes that Christina and Katie didn't quite understand.

"Very funny," Molly sneered, narrowing her sea-green eyes at Katie. "I do *not* look like Heidi. This is the latest look from Milan, if you must know. My mother brought this outfit back from the Italian spring preview shows."

Katie laughed a dismissive, who-cares laugh. "Oh, excuse me."

"You look good," Christina put in sincerely. "If I wore that outfit I'd look like a moose, but that style really suits you."

"You would not," Molly protested loyally. "You could wear anything."

"Thanks." Christina smiled. Although Molly and everyone else considered her absolutely beautiful, Christina, herself, fretted about her height and large frame.

A look of alarm suddenly changed Molly's face. "Did you mean I can wear this outfit well because I'm so thin? I don't look too thin to you, do I?"

"No, no," Christina quickly assured her. "I didn't mean anything like that. You just have the perfect body to carry off this look."

"That's true." Ashley added her vote of confidence. Molly's struggle with anorexia—the disease that had caused her to starve herself nearly to the point of dying—was well known to all of them. Lately, though, she'd been winning her daily battle to eat properly. Still thin, Molly kept her weight at a healthy level. But she had to be careful not to slip back into her old way of thinking. She didn't want to land back in the hospital.

The girls walked together down the hall toward their homeroom. Christina filled Katie and Molly in on all the scrumptious details she could recall about Dar Barrington.

"If you had seen the way he looked at Ashley, you'd know he really likes her," Christina gushed.

Ashley listened, feeling painfully self-conscious, but also thrilled to hear it all retold. Truthfully, Christina could have narrated the story a hundred more times and Ashley would have been delighted to hear it each time.

"I wonder when he'll call you," Molly said as they walked into homeroom, convinced that Dar would call Ashley. "Will your parents let you go out with him? He's kind of old for you."

"I don't know," Ashley admitted, taking her seat by the window. "I doubt it will be a problem because he's not going to ask me out."

She just couldn't dare to believe any of it might be true. Dar was much older, so popular. So gorgeous! Why get excited about something that couldn't possibly happen?

"Why wouldn't he ask you?" Molly challenged. "It sounds as if he really likes you."

"He'll ask her," Christina stated confidently before veering off to her assigned seat on the other side of the room.

Katie took her seat behind Ashley. "Remember, when Mr. Wonderful calls, I get the scoop for the paper," she teased.

"Ha! Ha!" Ashley replied dryly.

Darrin Tyson turned around in his seat in front of Ashley. "When who calls?" asked the large boy, brushing his hand along the top of his blond buzz cut. Darrin was a pain, but Ashley had known him for years and never took him seriously.

"Turn around, Darrin," she said in a barely tolerant big-sister tone. The last thing she needed was for Darrin to find out about Dar. She'd never hear the end of it.

"I know, the love of your life is calling you," Darrin taunted. He pretended to rub tears from his eyes. "And I thought I was the love of your life."

"You're the pain of my life," Ashley told him lightly.

"Gee, thanks," Darrin replied with a goofy smile.

"You're welcome," Ashley said, rolling her eyes. Darrin turned forward in his seat, and Ashley casually glanced toward the front door. "Oh, my gosh," she murmured softly.

The boy they'd almost hit yesterday—what was his name, again? Jason . . . something. Jason . . . something . . . had just walked into her homeroom class. The right lens of his taped black-framed glasses still showed the long, jagged crack from when they'd fallen on the road yesterday.

Christina turned in her seat, staring at Ashley with a surprised expression. Ashley met Christina's questioning eyes and shrugged. *What's he doing here?* Ashley wondered.

Her mind raced. Was the boy searching for her? Was it about the accident?

No, he took a seat toward the front of the classroom just as the late bell rang. He was joining the class. No wonder she'd never seen him before. He was obviously new in town.

Mr. Palmero, their homeroom teacher, asked the boy to stand up. "Class, I'd like you to meet Jason Hudson," Mr. Palmero said warmly. "Jason will be with us for the rest of the school year."

The boy slowly stood and blushed a deep pink as the class studied him. "H-H-Hi," he stammered with a quivering, forced smile.

He sure is a geek, Ashley thought, *but sweet-looking.* His shyness was somehow endearing. He so obviously struggled hard not to be shy. She could see that in the effort he made to smile at the class. That took guts, she decided.

Somehow, Jason Hudson brought out kindly, nurturing feelings in her. Maybe it was because he looked so helpless and lost. She approached him as she left homeroom and headed for her first class. "Hi, I'm Ashley Kingsley. You don't know me, but I've seen you before," she began.

"You . . . you . . . h-have?" Jason asked.

She quickly explained how Jeremy had almost hit

him yesterday and how she and Christina had been in the car.

The embarrassed red blush swept back into the boy's face. "Gosh . . . gosh, I'm s-s-sorry about . . . about that. I was th-th-thinking a-about something and I just didn't look. Good th-thing that deer ran into the road. Your brother said th-that's why he s-s-stopped. I h-h-hope his car is o-okay."

"It's fine," Ashley told him, smiling. *Poor guy,* she thought. *What an awful stutter.* "It wasn't your fault. Jeremy didn't brake for you, he braked because the deer jumped in front of his car."

Christina had come along just behind Ashley. "Only it wasn't a deer," she put in. "It was an angel. Your guardian angel, probably."

"My . . . my . . . what?" Jason's eyes grew wide.

"An angel," Christina repeated. "You see, it just looked like a deer because they do that sometimes. Angels can change into almost anything. I'm not sure why but—"

"We'd better be going now," Ashley cut Christina off abruptly. "We don't want to make Jason late for his first class."

"Why did you interrupt me?" Christina whispered hotly as Ashley ushered her toward the door.

"He'll think you're nuts," Ashley whispered back. "Think about it. We just met him. You can't start your very first conversation with this new kid by telling him his guardian angel saved him. We don't even know if he believes in angels."

At the door, Ashley turned back to ask Jason if he

needed help finding his way to class. At the same time, Darrin jostled the new boy as he joined a group of kids headed for the door.

Jason lunged forward. As he tried to grasp a desk to steady himself, his glasses fell from his face onto the floor. Ashley looked on in horror as Darrin's foot pressed down heavily on the glasses.

Crunch.

Had Darrin intentionally bumped into Jason?

It looked that way to Ashley. Leave it to Darrin to deliberately try to be obnoxious to someone new! It was so typical! He'd done it to Katie when she first came to Pine Ridge.

Ashley scowled darkly at Darrin.

Darrin returned Ashley's accusing stare with an expression of exaggerated innocence. "Oops!" he said loudly as he looked at the crunched eyeglasses under his big, booted foot. "Sorry, new kid." He didn't sound one bit sorry.

Jason fumbled on the floor, searching blindly for his glasses.

Ashley stooped for the mangled frames. "Here," she said, handing them to Jason.

"Th-thanks," Jason said as he tried to fit the crushed glasses onto his face.

"Can you see anything out of those?" Ashley asked, concerned.

"Not much," Jason admitted.

Ashley put her hand on his arm. "Come on. I'll help you find your class."

4

"Where do you live, Jason?" Ashley asked as she guided him onto the crowded school bus that afternoon. He groped the seat backs, straining to see clearly through the shattered lenses of his bent, broken glasses.

Ahead of them, Christina slipped into an empty seat first. She reached out and pulled Jason in beside her. Ashley wedged into the seat with them. "I have a brother named Jason," she said, trying to make conversation. "They're twins, Jeremy and Jason. I've always liked that name."

"Th-thanks," Jason mumbled, not looking at her.

"Where's your stop?" she asked again.

"Um . . . in . . . in town," he replied.

"Where in town?" Christina questioned him.

"Oh. Um . . . uh . . . th-the end. Toward the end."

Christina leaned forward to talk to Ashley across Jason. "Probably the stop by Pine Ridge Hardware," she suggested. "It's the last stop in town."

"Th-that's it," Jason confirmed eagerly. "Th-that's the one."

"Good," Ashley said. "We'll get off with you and help you home."

"No!" Jason cried. Realizing his overreaction, he softened his tone. "No. I mean, th-that's okay, really. Th-then you won't have a ride home yours-s-selves. I'll be f-fine."

"Give me a break, Jason," Ashley told him. "You can't see two inches in front of you with your glasses all messed up like that. How are you ever going to get home?"

"It's no . . . no big d-d-deal," he insisted.

"We don't mind helping you," Ashley assured him. "My brothers, Jason and Jeremy, are usually somewhere in town around this time. I'll find them at the diner or the pizzeria and catch a ride with them."

"What . . . what about you, Christina?" Jason asked.

"I live with her," Christina informed him. "We both live at the Pine Manor Ranch. Her parents own it, and my mother works there. We live in a cottage on the ranch. It's about five stops past town."

"It s-sounds nice," Jason noted wistfully.

"It is," Christina agreed. "It's the best. The ranch is on the other side of the Pine Manor Woods. You know, the woods you were biking out of yesterday." Christina frowned, remembering. "What were you doing in the woods, anyway?"

"Nothing," Jason replied too quickly.

"Nothing?" Christina questioned.

"Just riding my bike," he explained.

Ashley and Christina exchanged skeptical glances. "You were riding your bike in the woods?" Ashley eyed Jason suspiciously. "Isn't that sort of difficult, especially in winter? Don't you bump into rocks and bang into roots and all?"

"Not really," Jason answered with an anxious laugh. "It's f-f-fun when you get the h-h-hang of it. It's a ch-challenge t-to stay on th-the b-b-bike."

"I suppose," Ashley conceded, unconvinced. Why was Jason so nervous? It seemed as if he was hiding something from them. Was he ashamed of where he lived? Did he even have a place to live?

They rode through downtown Pine Ridge, a small, quiet commercial area with low brick buildings. "Here's your stop," Christina noted as the bus slowed in front of Pine Ridge Hardware.

Jason jumped up. "Bye. S-see you to-tomorrow." As he pushed past Ashley, he tripped over her foot and fell, face first, into the muddy aisle. The bus exploded with laughter.

Ashley and Christina leaped from their seats to help him. "Jason, let us go with you," Ashley pleaded, brushing off his jacket.

Jason pulled away from her. "Th-thank you, but I'm f-fine." Using the seat backs as his guide, he made his way to the front of the bus.

"He's so odd," Ashley said to Christina when the bus doors had folded shut. "Did you get the idea he was hiding something?"

"Definitely," Christina concurred.

Peering out the window, the girls watched Jason turn in bewildered circles on the street corner. "He has no idea where he is," Ashley observed as the bus pulled away from the curb and veered toward the road that led past the Pine Manor Woods.

One stop later, kids who lived in a cluster of homes across from the stately pines were getting off. "We should go back for him." Ashley spoke her thoughts. "We can't just leave him there."

"I've been thinking the same thing," Christina admitted. "Let's go."

The girls scrambled off the bus just as the doors were closing. If they walked briskly, they could be back in town in a little over five minutes. The poor near-sighted kid would probably still be turning circles on the corner, Ashley assumed. She felt somehow responsible for him, even though he refused the help she offered.

"Wow, it's getting cold," Christina commented, pulling her purple woolen cape more tightly around herself. "I hate this time of year. It's so cold and spring seems so far away."

"I know," Ashley agreed, jamming her hands into the deep, warm pockets of her gold parka. They continued along the narrow dirt edge between the piney woods and the road, the occasional car zooming past. The heavy, snow-laden evergreens seemed to whisper secrets as their rich green branches brushed against one another.

Christina walked just ahead of Ashley, since there wasn't enough room for the girls to walk side by side. As they hurried along, Ashley's thoughts wandered, first to Dar. In minutes she was daydreaming of his smile, his gorgeous square-jawed face. Then her thoughts drifted back to Jason.

Funny, but seeing him without glasses earlier today in school made him look entirely different. Some nearsighted people looked sort of blank and bewildered without their glasses. Not Jason. His hazel eyes were lively, as if they flared with an inner light as he gazed at people.

Christina stopped so abruptly that Ashley bumped into her. "Look," Christina murmured, awestruck, reaching back to clutch Ashley's arm.

Ashley drew in a sharp, astonished breath.

Jason was approaching them. Why wasn't he in town? Was he totally lost? Or had he lied to them about where he lived?

He'd picked up a big stick and was using it as a blind person would use a cane, sweeping it before him as he walked.

But that wasn't what amazed Ashley and Christina.

Behind Jason, walking with him, was a gorgeous sunlight-drenched angel—the same angel that had swept Jeremy's car aside with one movement of his powerful hand. The angel's arm was linked through Jason's, guiding him, keeping him off the road.

"How beautiful," Christina said, her expression and tone filled with awe.

A car sped by without slowing.

Jason stepped off the narrow dirt path, veering toward the car.

Ashley's hands flew to her face as she drew a sharp, frightened breath. She stared blankly ahead as the car closed in on Jason.

The angel gently tugged the boy back to the side of the road. Jason cocked his head toward the whoosh of the rapidly passing car and froze. Ashley saw his shoulders shake as a shiver ran through him. He realized he'd had a close call.

"Whew!" Christina gasped.

Ashley watched the car drive on without even slowing. She expected the driver to at least stop to check on Jason, but he didn't. Hadn't the driver even noticed the huge, wildly luminous angel walking beside the road?

Apparently not.

"Jason and the angel are heading right toward us." Ashley spoke urgently, her hand on Christina's shoulder. "What should we do? What should we say to him? Should we tell Jason there's an angel with him? Do you think he knows?"

Before Christina could reply, Jason and the angel turned into the woods. "Why are they heading into the woods?" Ashley wondered aloud. "Where are they going?"

"To the Angels Crossing Bridge?" Christina suggested quietly. Her eyes were glued to the spot where the angel had saved Jason's life.

"Maybe," Ashley agreed. After all, Jason was with an angel. Perhaps the angel was leading him to the bridge. But why?

Ashley decided there was only one way to find out what was going on. "Come on, let's follow them."

5

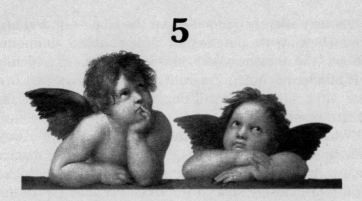

"They've disappeared," Christina observed. The girls had followed Jason and the angel several yards into the woods. But a leaping squirrel had startled them, making them look away for only a moment. When they looked back, Jason and the angel were gone.

"The angel could disappear, but not Jason," Ashley insisted. "He's got to be here somewhere. Let's head for the bridge. We'll probably catch up with him."

The girls didn't usually enter the woods from this direction. Most of the time they entered from behind the horse stable on the ranch. From there, they easily knew their way to the Angels Crossing Bridge. But now they weren't entirely sure where they stood in relation to the bridge.

"I think it might be this way," Christina said. She headed down a steep slope carpeted with fallen brown pine needles that had accumulated on the ground through the passing of uncountable years.

As they silently padded down the slope—dotted here and there with patches of pine-studded, unmelted snow—the ancient woods enveloped them in a blanket of thunderous quiet. Fragrant pine scents washed over the girls, filling them, lifting their spirits. Energizing them somehow.

Whenever she entered these woods, Ashley always felt that she was moving into some timeless, magical place. And the deeper inside she ventured—the thicker and more closely spaced the trees became, the farther she went from the edges of the woods—the more intense the timeless feeling grew. It was nearly indescribable, but so real. She would lose her usually keen sense of how much time had passed. She might be in the woods five minutes or five hours. She could never be sure.

Ashley checked her watch. It had stopped. Just as it always did when she reached a certain point in the woods.

"Mine stopped, too," Christina said as she glanced from Ashley's wrist to her own. "That's a good sign. Our watches always stop when we're nearing the bridge."

They moved through a thick stand of birch trees, shimmering as the wind ruffled their papery white bark. "I remember these birches," Christina recalled. "There should be waterfalls around here somewhere."

"That's right," Ashley recalled. She froze and listened. "I hear them. Come on."

Running toward the sound of rushing water, they came to a sparkling waterfall that cascaded into a crystal pool and then poured out again in a second waterfall on the other side. "The power spot," Christina said excitedly, stepping to the edge of the pool.

They'd been here before. Christina believed this woods was full of sacred places where positive energy collected and exerted a strong force over everything that came in contact with it. It was a good force and incredibly strong.

Not only that, she believed it was a place where the spirit world could contact this one. A crossover spot. She was sure this was a power spot—and that the Angels Crossing Bridge was another one.

Ashley looked up at the towering pines surrounding the pool. She wanted to see if all the birds that had crowded the area in summer, when last they'd visited there, were still around. At first, it seemed they'd left.

The sharp call of a blue jay soon made her look more closely. The large, vivid blue bird darted from one treetop to the next. Its movement irritated a flurry of other winter birds. The small gray titmouse. A brilliant red cardinal, followed by his drab green wife. Sparrows, finches, and other small brownish birds. A chickadee landed on a pine branch next to Ashley and cheerfully trilled *chick-a-dee-dee-dee*.

"This place is still bird world," Ashley observed happily, glad to see that the area teemed with life despite the deadness of winter.

An unexplainable joy welled up inside her, as if the good energy from the spot was already working its wonders. Or maybe it was just the cheery, calling birds and the burbling, rushing water lifting the winter chill from her spirit.

"Come on," Christina urged. "I know where we are now. If we follow this stream from the second waterfall, it will lead us right to the bridge."

The stream water ran lower than in spring and summer. Rocks jutted out in the middle. The girls followed it until a wooden, covered bridge came into view.

They stopped to look at it. No matter how often they saw it, the bridge always filled them with excitement. What would they find this time?

6

The splintered wooden boards groaned under Ashley's and Christina's boots as they stepped onto the dilapidated bridge. Waist-high sides enclosed the bottom half of the structure. On the top half, thick, hand-carved wooden bracings held up the roof and were the only things that partially obscured the view. On both sides the girls saw the path of a rushing creek full of small rocky descents that created silvery waterfalls where the water tumbled past.

Ashley slapped her forehead as the high whine of a mosquito filled her ears. "A mosquito in winter?" she questioned.

"Careful!" a voice warned from out of nowhere.

Christina and Ashley looked all around, bewildered. No one was there.

Two butterflies fluttered past, one yellow, one orange, and lighted on a crossbeam near the top, where the two sides of the bridge's peaked roof met.

The girls looked at one another, puzzled. When they looked back, they gasped with surprise. Two female angels sat on the side of the bridge, dangling their robed legs from the beam. One was a gorgeous blond woman, with abundant shoulder-length curls and golden wings. The other had more angular features and waist-long, silky black hair. Both had the striking, unusual lavender-blue eyes the girls had seen in most angels.

They knew these two well. Edwina was the blond one. Norma, the dark-haired angel. "You almost smooshed Ned," Edwina informed them.

"Ned?" Ashley asked, looking around for the third angel who often appeared at the bridge. "Smooshed him? Where?"

She heard the droning buzz again.

"He's on your ear," Norma put in, floating effortlessly to the ground.

"He's a mosquito?" Ashley cried, instinctively shaking her head.

Edwina giggled under her breath and followed Norma down. "Yes, and it looks like he's going to be one for quite some time."

The buzzing grew angry, and Ashley jumped back as Ned whizzed by.

"Don't worry," Norma said, perching on the side of the bridge with the ease of a bird on a telephone wire. "Ned would never hurt you. He's just mad."

"Why is he mad?" Christina asked.

"He's stuck," Edwina said, then laughed, a high bell-like sound. "That's what he gets for showing off."

"You see," Norma explained, "we had this problem to solve. We're looking after this lovely, but very poor, family in Mexico. Their new baby is highly allergic to bee stings, only the family doesn't know it yet. If the baby is stung by a bee, she'll die."

"And there's a hive being built in a tree right outside the baby's window, but the parents don't realize that yet, either," Edwina added. "The other thing they aren't aware of is that there's a small tear in the window screen in the baby's room."

"Oh, no!" Christina gasped, covering her mouth in horror at the potential danger.

"Exactly," Norma said with a knowing nod.

"We didn't know how to warn the parents about all of these things, so we went to the angel casebook," Edwina continued. "And there we saw a section on insecttransmorphication."

"What?" Ashley asked.

"Instructions that tell angels how to change into bugs," Norma supplied.

"It's extremely hard to do," Edwina revealed, her voice barely a whisper. "Advanced, first-class angels with centuries of experience have trouble with it. You'd think it would be easy, considering that we already have the wings. But shrinking is just so difficult."

"You did it, though," Christina pointed out. "Congratulations."

Edwina and Norma smiled at one another. "We did, didn't we?" Edwina said, delighted. "It was fun, too. Butterfly wings have a completely different feel. You just gently flap your feathery wings and glide along on the breeze." She shut her eyes and spread her arms, recapturing the sensation of butterfly flight.

"But changing into butterflies is fairly easy," Norma admitted frankly. "Mr. Big Shot over there had to try to change into a mosquito. The very hardest one there is."

"Well, he did it," Ashley pointed out.

"That's true," Edwina said, opening her eyes and bringing her arms down to her sides. "Norma, you have to admit Ned's plan was rather good."

"Yes," Norma conceded with a thoughtful tilt of her head. "He was such a pesky bug, bouncing off the walls, whining so loudly. The father and mother just couldn't ignore him. They started looking around to see how he got in, and that's when they discovered the torn window screen. Right away, the father sent the wife to get some wire so he could mend it."

"What did you do?" Christina asked.

"We had the easy job," Edwina told them. "There's a doctor who lives one town over. He collects butterflies. He was out in a nearby field with his net, and we led him on a merry chase right to the front porch of our family.

"That's where he met the wife, who had come out on the porch to search for the wire. She and the doctor started chatting. When she found out the man was a doctor, she pointed out the baby's rash," Edwina continued. "The doctor offered to come back with his bag and give the baby a thorough checkup and some shots. The rash will turn out to be an allergy to milk. The doctor will test for other allergies and discover the one to bees. The family will check all around for bees, discover the hive, and remove it."

"All right," Christina cheered, pumping the air. "Way to go!"

Norma and Edwina grinned at one another. "It was one of our trickier maneuvers, but it's working beautifully," Norma agreed.

An angry buzzing echoed loudly on the bridge.

"We haven't forgotten you, Ned," Edwina said sympathetically. "We simply don't know what to do. Concentrate on changing back. That's what we did, and it worked."

More angry buzzing.

"Well, concentrate harder, then," Norma told him impatiently.

The buzzing turned into a high, frantic whine. A baseball-sized burst of light exploded in the middle of the bridge, where Ned had been only seconds earlier.

Christina and Ashley were momentarily blinded, as if someone had snapped a flashbulb in their eyes. When they could see again, Ned lay crumpled in the corner of the bridge, looking as if he had collided headfirst with one of the heavy crossbeams that supported the bridge's sagging roof.

It was hard not to laugh. His ash-blond hair stood on end like a cartoon of someone who'd stuck his finger in an electrical outlet. Ned's large wings lay bent at odd angles, and his angel robe was wrapped around him as if he'd tried to put it on during a tornado.

Norma yelped with laughter. "Welcome back."

Slowly, with an expression of injured dignity, Ned rose to his feet and carefully began to straighten his wings. He smoothed his hair, then stumbled backward, still dizzy.

Edwina floated to him and took his elbow. "Are you okay? That was great work."

"Thank you," Ned replied. "Piece of cake." As he spoke, he stumbled over his tangled robe and collapsed into the side of the bridge.

This obvious lie with its accompanying pratfall sent them all into gales of laughter. "It was!" Ned insisted indignantly. "Well, next time it will be. I was just getting the hang of being a bug this time. Next time will be a snap."

"Will there be a next time?" Norma asked, still panting with laughter.

"Not soon, I hope," Ned admitted, smiling as he righted himself. "Not soon." He looked at Christina and Ashley. "What brings you two ladies here today?"

"A boy," Ashley began, then she went on to explain about Jason and how they'd followed him and an angel into the woods. "We thought the angel might bring him here for some reason."

"We've been out of the country most of the day," Edwina said. "We haven't seen anyone here in the last few minutes since we've been back."

"Where do you think the angel was taking him?" Ashley persisted.

Edwina shrugged. "We haven't been in touch with the

others. Communications are difficult when you're in bug form."

"Could you contact that angel now?" Ashley pressed.

"Is this boy a friend of yours?" Norma inquired.

"No," Ashley admitted. "Not really."

"Do you care about him, or are you simply being nosy?" Ned asked.

Ashley looked to Christina, who appeared equally perplexed by the question. "I'm not sure," Ashley confessed.

"You have to find out," Norma stated matter-of-factly. "It makes a huge difference, you know."

As she spoke, a loud alarm began beeping. It came from the black watch on Norma's wrist.

7

"I hate when they leave so suddenly like that," Ashley griped as she and Christina walked through the darkening woods toward the ranch. At the sound of Norma's beeping watch, the angels had bid the girls a quick good-bye and almost instantly disappeared.

"That watch alarm tells them they have to be somewhere," Christina reminded her.

Ashley laughed lightly. "Yeah. Somewhere like ancient Rome or Colonial America." They knew the angels moved swiftly not only through space, but also through time.

They continued on until the faded red wall of the stable showed through the trees. Ashley was suddenly aware that her feet ached from the long walk. The superenergized feeling she usually got from the woods was beginning to fade. The hands on her watch once again began to move.

A few minutes later they were walking around the side of the stable into the heart of the Pine Manor

Ranch. "Hi, girls!" A tall woman wearing faded jeans and a heavy quilted work jacket waved to them with a gloved hand. It was Alice, Christina's mother. She worked as a ranch hand, trail ride leader, and riding instructor at the ranch.

The girls waved back. "See you tomorrow," Christina told Ashley as she headed toward her mother.

"See ya." Ashley headed quickly across the wide dirt road to her low, pale yellow ranch-style house on the other side.

Another woman, petite with short, reddish hair, came out onto the house's porch and petted a sleeping golden retriever. "Hi, Ashley. How come you're late?" Mrs. Kingsley asked.

"We came home through the woods," Ashley replied, coming up onto the porch.

Her mother's face clouded with concern. "Why did you go that way?"

Ashley explained about the new boy and how she and Christina had gone to the bridge looking for him. She told her mother about their encounter with the angels.

Mrs. Kingsley had been skeptical about the angels, but now believed that there were angels in the woods, although she had never seen them. "It was weird, Mom," Ashley went on. "Jason could barely see, yet he went into the woods. He was in the woods the other day, too."

"Didn't you tell me once that there was a family living on the far side of the woods? Doesn't Christina know them?" her mother recalled. "Maybe this boy is staying with them."

"That family moved into town a while ago," Ashley told her. "I wonder if Jason's family lives in that house now?" The small house was deep in the woods. Christina had discovered it and the family while walking in the woods one day. The idea that Jason had a warm place to live made Ashley less worried about him. It explained a lot. But why would he lie about it? She was sure there was some mystery about him.

Her mother went out to the stable to tell her father something. Ashley went into the house and plunked herself in front of the television in the living room, snapping it on with the remote. Stretching her legs out in front of her, she felt them throb from all the walking she and Christina had done.

Leaning forward, she massaged her right calf, which was starting to cramp. As she kneaded the tight muscle, she thought about Norma's words. Was she Jason's friend, or just nosy? A busybody, as her mother called it.

"Nosy," she murmured. It was the truth, after all. But maybe not. Ashley liked Jason, although she didn't really know him yet. Perhaps she would truly be his friend someday.

What was Norma actually trying to say? That Ashley shouldn't barge into Jason's life unless she intended to be a friend? That was probably true.

The kitchen phone rang. Ashley waited for several rings, hoping that one of her brothers would get it. On the fourth ring, she reluctantly pulled herself from her comfortable chair and hobbled toward the cheerful yellow kitchen. "Hello?" she said, snapping up the phone.

"This is Dar Barrington. Is Ashley there?"

Ashley's heart slammed into her breastbone. She couldn't breathe. Her hands trembled.

Then her eyes narrowed suspiciously. Was this some kind of joke?

"This is Ashley," she replied cautiously.

"Hi, I'm glad I caught you." It sounded like Dar, as best she could remember his voice—his wonderful, rich voice. It *had* to be him, she decided. No one could imitate that voice.

She pulled over a kitchen chair and fell heavily into it. Her knees were suddenly as wobbly as Jell-O. "What's up?" she asked, desperate to sound casual, yet aware of a mortifying quaver in her tone.

"Listen, thanks a lot for throwing the gig our way," he went on.

"Sure. No problem. You guys are great." Ashley nervously pinched the palm of her left hand and noticed it kept her voice steadier.

"We're going to rehearse at the middle school tomorrow. You know, get the feel of the space and adjust our sound system to it. I was wondering if you want to come hear us."

Ashley's heart banged in her chest. "I'd love to!" *Did that sound too eager?* she wondered. "I mean, sounds good," she amended more coolly.

Was this just an official-business kind of call, or was it something more personal, as she hoped? "Should I call Rachel and ask her to join us?" she asked, testing.

"No, don't call her," he replied. "The truth is, I just really want to see you again."

"You do?" she said, breathlessly.

"Yeah."

"What time should I be there?"

"We'll start around five and probably go to seven or so. So, I'll see you there?"

"Uh-huh. I'll be there."

"Great. Bye."

"Bye." Ashley replaced the receiver on the hook. Had that just really happened? Had Dar Barrington really called her at home? Yes. "Yes!" she cheered, pumping the air with her fist as she jumped around the kitchen.

"Yes! Yes! Yes!"

Wait! Ashley froze with her arm in the air. She was supposed to have a sleepover at Christina's house tomorrow night. Slowly lowering her arm, she plunked into a chair. Well, she'd just have to get out of the sleepover. Her friends would understand.

But how would she get to the middle school? Would Jeremy or Jason drive her? Would her parents even let her go?

Ashley's mother came into the kitchen. "Who was on the phone?"

"Um . . ." She had to be sure to present this in the right way. Her parents only allowed group dates. If they thought she was going just to be near some boy, they'd never understand. "That was . . . the dance committee," she lied. "They want me to go to school tomorrow night to check out a band."

"I thought you already settled on one," her mother said, taking wrapped frozen meat from the freezer.

"We did but . . . it's not final. Tomorrow they'll decide for sure. I have to be there. Have to!"

"I thought you and your friends were going to sleep at Christina's and work on your science fair projects."

"I'll have to cancel out of that. This is super important."

"Not more important than your schoolwork," her mother said, unwrapping a chicken. Her expression softened. "All right. I know how hard you've been working on the dance. I'll drive you over to school. Maybe I'll stay and listen to the band with you."

"No!" Ashley shrieked. Her mother turned and looked at her, surprised by her daughter's intense reaction. Ashley lowered her voice. "I mean . . . you know how it is, Mom."

Mrs. Kingsley smiled. "Yes. I was young once, too. I remember. You don't want your mother hanging around."

"No offense," Ashley said quickly.

"It's all right."

Whew. Now she had a ride.

"How long will you be there?" her mother asked.

"Well, they're supposed to start at five, and they'll probably be done around seven," Ashley replied.

"I suppose you could go to Christina's when you come back," Mrs. Kingsley suggested. "You'll still have a few hours to work on your project."

"That's true," Ashley agreed. Everything was working out perfectly. Tomorrow she'd watch Dar perform. He'd smile at her as he sang, so glad she'd come to see him. Then who knew what would happen from there?

8

"Jason! Jason, wait!" Ashley ran down the hall after Jason in school the next morning.

He stopped and squinted in her direction. He wasn't wearing his glasses. Ashley thought he looked much better without them. Almost good-looking.

When she was an arm's length away, he smiled. "H-hi, Ashley."

"Did you get home all right yesterday?" she asked.

"Yes. I told you th-there was nothing to worry about."

She studied him a moment, then decided to be direct. "Christina and I saw you go into the woods. Do you live there?"

Jason instantly colored with embarrassment. "Uh . . . yes, I do." The bell for homeroom sounded. "I'd better go," he said, clearly eager to escape this conversation.

Ashley trailed after him. "I'll help you get to class," she offered. "I know it's hard for you to see."

"Th-thanks," Jason accepted, turning an even deeper

shade of red. She took his arm and guided him toward homeroom.

"Where did you live before moving to Pine Ridge?" she asked.

"Miller's Creek," he said, naming the next town over.

"Why did you move to Pine Ridge?"

He mumbled something so softly that Ashley couldn't hear. "Excuse me?" she asked as they stopped in front of their homeroom class. "I didn't hear what you said."

"Angels," he repeated more loudly.

"You moved here because of angels?" Ashley echoed, astonished.

Gently pulling free of her grasp, he held onto the door jamb. "It's too crazy to explain. F-forget it." He smiled shyly. "Th-thanks for the help." He lurched inside, knocking into a desk as he went.

"If you're not careful, he's going to think you like him," warned Molly, coming up alongside Ashley.

"I *do* like him," Ashley replied.

"You know what I mean," Molly scolded, twisting her hair into a coil and then letting it spin free. "You're spending an awful lot of time hanging around him. He's going to get the wrong idea."

"What are you saying?" Ashley challenged. "Why can't I be nice to Jason even though I don't want him for a boyfriend?"

"You can be nice, but you don't have to act so interested," Molly said calmly. "I saw you chasing him down the hall just now. That kind of stuff can give a guy the wrong impression."

Ashley's hands flew to her hips. "I did *not* chase him down the hall. I was running to catch up with him. Is that so bad?"

"It's not bad, but it's going to give him the wrong idea," Molly insisted.

"Jason knows he's not the kind of guy girls like . . . not in that way," Ashley said.

"That's crazy," Molly scoffed. "No one would think that about themselves."

"They wouldn't?" Ashley asked sheepishly.

"No," Molly said. "They wouldn't."

Although she knew there was some truth in what Molly said, something inside Ashley rebelled against it. Why should she stop being nice to Jason? Wasn't he a person? Wasn't she? Why couldn't they just be people? Why did this boy-girl thing have to figure into it?

"He told me something interesting," Ashley said, changing the subject slightly. "He lives in the woods and he's there because of angels."

"What does that mean?" Molly wondered.

"I don't know yet, but I'm going to find out."

9

At five o'clock that evening, Ashley stepped into the middle school cafeteria, feeling awkward. *I'm the co-chairperson of the dance committee*, she reminded herself. *I should be here.*

She knew that was so. But she couldn't get over the feeling that she looked like a girl with a gigantic crush chasing the rock and roll star of her dreams.

Stop it! She scolded herself. She wasn't chasing him. He'd invited her. Ashley quickly took in the scene in the cafeteria.

Dar stood with his band members, who were busy setting up their equipment. The moment he noticed her at the back of the room, he smiled and waved. She waved back. A rush of excitement swept through her. He looked so glad to see her.

Other girls were there. All of them older, in high school, probably. Friends of the band, she guessed. Ashley felt very young as she neared their group. They eyed her casually, with only mild interest, then turned back to their conversation.

Leaving the band, Dar walked over to her. "Wow! I'm so glad you came, Ashley."

"Me, too," Ashley replied, smiling more broadly than she intended.

Dar pulled one of the folding metal chairs out for her. "Have a seat," he said gallantly. "We'll start to play in a second."

"Cool," Ashley said, smiling up at him as she sat. He returned to the band. When they had completed their sound checks, the group played a song that was popular on the radio, then another Dar had written. It was titled "Hey, Beautiful One, Who Are You?"

"I just wrote this one." Dar gazed at Ashley as he spoke into the microphone. "This is the first time we're doing it."

The band played the first few notes, then Dar began to sing the romantic song. The words spoke of being in love with a girl he hardly knew, about thinking of her all the time.

Ashley leaned forward on the chair, melting at the sound of his voice. He caught her eye and smiled. With an excited shiver, she dared to wonder if he'd written it for her. He could have.

The words fit.

At that moment, he was certainly singing it directly to her. That much was very obvious.

With a sidelong glance, she secretively looked at the high school girls sitting several feet away. They were staring at her with new interest. Ashley looked away quickly. Inside, she swelled with pride as she fought down an excited smile.

They couldn't dismiss her now. Dar Barrington was obviously interested in her. Ashley Kingsley—mere eighth grader—had won over the most popular boy at Pine Ridge High.

When the set ended, Dar came right up to her. "What did you think?"

"It was awesome," she complimented him honestly. "Completely awesome."

Dar smiled, pleased. "Thanks." He shifted anxiously from one foot to the other. "Can I give you a ride home?"

Her brother, Jeremy, was coming to pick her up on his way home from work. But how could she turn down a chance to be alone with Dar? Jeremy would understand. The school was only a couple of minutes out of his way.

"Sure," she replied. "Do you have a car?"

"Yeah. I just need to help break down the equipment and we can go."

Ashley hugged herself gleefully as Dar returned to the band. This was so cool. So totally cool.

Not wanting the high school girls to see her smiling like a fool, Ashley turned toward the door at the back of the cafeteria.

Oh, no! she gasped silently.

Jeremy stood in the doorway about to step into the room.

She ducked below the top of a table. If he saw her, she'd have to leave with him.

From beneath the table, she could see him walking farther in. What if he asked someone where she was? What if she had to crawl out from under the table in front of everyone? She shouldn't have come under here. But what else could she have done?

Ashley held her breath as she watched Jeremy search the cafeteria for her. One of the girls from the high school group walked near him. He was going to ask her.

With her hands clasped in horror over her mouth, Ashley watched. The girl shook her head. No, she didn't know where Ashley was.

Whew!

Frowning, Jeremy left the cafeteria. Ashley exhaled with a whoosh of relief. That could have been *so* embarrassing. She decided to stay down a few more minutes in case he came back.

She was still squatting below the table when she sensed a presence behind her. Turning and looking up, she saw Dar gazing down at her. "Is something wrong?" he asked.

"Uh . . ." she stammered. "Uh . . ."

Don't you dare blush, she commanded herself. "My contact lens," she lied in a sudden burst of inventiveness. "I dropped it."

He knelt down beside her. "I'll help you look."

They were so close, nearly touching. Ashley's heart pounded.

"Are you sure you dropped it here?" Dar asked after several minutes of searching.

"Maybe not," Ashley replied. They couldn't crawl on the ground forever. "Forget it. I have an extra set at home."

"Okay. If you're sure?" Dar agreed, standing.

"Absolutely. No big deal." She followed Dar out to his old car, parked behind the school. Ashley felt bad about dodging Jeremy like that. He was always so nice about driving her places. She felt bad, too, about the contact lens lie.

But as she slipped into the front seat next to Dar, all those concerns disappeared. She felt grown-up and beautiful—already a sophisticated high school girl.

She told him where she lived, and he headed toward the ranch. "I can't believe you're only in eighth grade," he said, stopping at a light in town. "You seem so much older. What are you, fourteen?"

"Yeah," she lied, again. She wouldn't be fourteen until next October.

"You have a lot of self-assurance," he went on as the light changed to green. "Isn't it funny that you seem older than a lot of girls I know in school, even though you're younger?"

"I suppose," Ashley said, not really knowing how to respond. His remarks weren't a complete surprise to her. All through school, teachers had commented on her maturity. It had always seemed to her like an incredibly boring compliment. Why couldn't she be brilliant? Or gorgeous? Or outrageously gifted at something? No, she was just mature. Big deal.

But now she was wildly thankful for possessing that

quality. If that was what Dar liked about her, then she'd be more mature than ever before.

"You're prettier than most of the girls I meet, too," Dar added.

The remark left her speechless.

For a second she thought she must have heard him wrong. Not that she didn't think she was pretty—pretty enough, anyway. She'd been told that before. But that *he* thought it—that he'd *said* it. Out loud! It was unbelievable.

Unbelievably wonderful!

"Thanks," she murmured, this time unable to control the hot blush that spread across her cheeks and over her forehead. She looked away, hoping that, in the darkness, he wouldn't see.

As she instructed, he turned right at a red barn and drove down the dirt road leading into the ranch. "It must be cool to live on a ranch," he commented admiringly.

"I don't know. I've always lived here. But I like it." At Christina's house, she told him to stop. "I'm meeting my friends here," she explained. The truth was, she would never let Dar drive her to her house. She knew her parents would freak if they saw her getting out of a strange boy's car.

"Ashley, would you mind if I called you sometime?" Dar asked. "We could go out and do something—just the two of us?"

She grabbed one hand with the other to keep them from shaking. "Sure. I'd like that."

He leaned forward and his lips brushed hers with a light kiss. Within her, everything shook. Quaked.

He'd kissed her!

"Good night," she said breathlessly, drawing gently away from his embrace, backing out of the car. "Thanks for the ride."

"You're welcome." He smiled warmly. "I'll call you."

Ashley stood in front of Christina's and waved, watching him drive away, smoke billowing from the exhaust pipe of his car.

A noise from behind made her turn. Christina, Molly, and Katie stood crowded together in the front window, lit from behind by the warm glow of a roaring fire in the stone fireplace.

In the next second, the front door flew open and the girls raced out to her. "He drove you home?" Molly gasped. "Was that Dar?"

Ashley nodded blissfully. "He kissed me good night," she whispered.

In unison, the girls screamed with excitement.

"I told you! I told you!" Christina exulted. "The tarot cards never lie!"

"Except when they're completely wrong," quipped Katie. Christina crossed her eyes comically in reply. She was used to Katie's continual skepticism.

"The *cards* are never wrong," Christina argued as the girls headed back into the cozy house. "The person reading them might misinterpret their meaning, but the cards themselves are always right."

"Yeah, sure," Katie grumbled doubtfully.

"Who cares about those silly tarot cards!" Molly cried impatiently. "I want to hear about Dar. Tell us everything. Everything!"

Smiling as she stepped into the house, Ashley told every detail, about how the high school girls had eyed her with such boredom and how their glances had grown into respectful stares when Dar began singing to her. She told about hiding from Jeremy and pretending to have lost her contact lens.

"What a hoot!" Molly laughed, clapping her hands giddily as she perched on the arm of the couch. "The two of you crawling around on the cafeteria floor. I can just picture it! But it sounds sort of romantic. Was it?"

"In a way," Ashley admitted, bright-eyed at the memory. "Then, when we were in the car together, he said he thought I was—"

"Wait a minute," Katie interrupted firmly. "Slow down. You hid from Jeremy?"

"Yeah," Ashley admitted sheepishly. "I know it wasn't nice but—"

"That means your parents don't know you're home," Katie pointed out. "He must have gone home and said he couldn't find you."

Ashley paled. "You're right." In all the excitement, she hadn't thought of that.

The phone rang in the kitchen. Christina reached over the counter that separated the cozy living room from the kitchen and snapped it up quickly. "Oh, hi, Mrs. Kingsley." She spoke nervously, staring at Ashley with panicked eyes.

"What do I say? What should I say?" Ashley asked Molly and Katie anxiously. They shrugged their shoulders in response.

"Yes, she's here," Christina said slowly. "Oh, you want to talk to her? Um . . . sure." She covered the phone and held it out to Ashley. "I didn't know what else to say," she whispered apologetically.

Her mother would probably be upset that Jeremy hadn't found her at school. She'd want to know where she'd been, how she'd gotten home. What could Ashley possibly say? How could she explain that she'd hidden from Jeremy so she could ride home with Dar?

Christina waved the phone at Ashley.

"Say I'm in the bathroom!" Ashley hissed, pushing the phone away. "I need to think."

Christina shook her head, unwilling to do it. Ashley had never heard Christina lie. She probably did it badly anyway, Ashley decided. Reluctantly, she took the phone from her friend.

"Uh . . . hi, Mom," she said with a nervous quaver in her voice.

"Ashley," her mother scolded fiercely. "Where on earth were you?"

10

"But, Mom," Ashley lied, glancing away from her mother's steely gaze. "I didn't see him."

It was only twenty minutes later. Her mother had insisted she come home from Christina's immediately. Their houses were just down the road from each other. Ashley wished the walk was longer. She needed time to figure out what to say.

"How could you not see Jeremy?" Mrs. Kingsley challenged skeptically, rising from the kitchen chair where she'd sat. "He said he walked right into the cafeteria."

"I don't know. Maybe I went into the girls' room or something."

"How did you get to Christina's?" her mother asked.

"One of the band members drove me," Ashley replied. There was no harm in telling that truth. Besides, Ashley couldn't think of a believable lie.

"A boy you don't know drove you home?" Mrs.

Kingsley questioned. "A high school boy?"

"Yes." Ashley squirmed in her chair. Her mother was clearly upset. Ashley could tell from the strained tone of her mother's voice and the two vertical scowl lines that had formed on her forehead at the middle of her brow. Ashley couldn't recall the last time her mother had been so angry at her.

Ashley and her petite redheaded mother looked so much alike. She wondered, for a moment, if she'd get lines like those when she was older.

Mrs. Kingsley sat back down. "Ashley," she said with a new, forced calmness. "I do not want you going in a car with a boy unless you have our permission."

"Why not?" Ashley cried indignantly. "I needed a ride and he was nice enough to give me one. I don't see the problem."

"That's our rule, Ashley," her mother countered, still calm. "I didn't think this would come up until you were in high school and old enough to go out on dates. But since it has come up, we have to talk about it. Unless your father and I know the boy and feel comfortable about his driving and his character, I don't want you taking rides."

"But, Mom," Ashley protested, rising in her seat.

"No buts. That's the rule," came a deep voice from the kitchen doorway. Ashley turned to see her tall, broad-shouldered father. His weathered face wore a serious expression. "I just came back from the middle school," he continued. "I was worried something happened to you."

"Sorry," Ashley apologized sincerely. She hadn't meant to worry them or make her father drive all the way to school. It hadn't even occurred to her. Her parents had been the furthest thing from her mind when Dar offered to drive her home.

"We trust you, Ashley," her mother said. "You've never given us a reason not to. But next time, call us if you need a ride. Someone will come for you."

"Okay," Ashley agreed.

"Good," her mother said. "Now please go to your room and finish your homework."

After a brief moment of silence, a question occurred to Ashley, which she just had to ask. "Mom, you said that in high school I'd be old enough to date. Does that mean you don't think I'm old enough now?"

"No, you're not old enough," her father declared firmly as he turned and left the kitchen.

She looked hopefully to her mother to give her a different answer. "We let you go out with that Trevor boy, but that was—"

"He turned out to be a jerk," Ashley cut in. "He doesn't count."

"My point is, we let you go out with him during the day and with a group of other kids. That kind of date is all right for now. We'd like you to wait until you're in high school for single dates."

"But that's just next year. What difference does a year make?" Ashley argued.

"Did someone ask you out?" Mrs. Kingsley asked.

"Not exactly, but I think he will," she admitted. "The

boy who drove me home asked if he could call me and I said yes."

Mrs. Kingsley shook her head. "Sorry, you're not old enough to go out alone with a boy, especially not one who already has his driver's license."

"That makes no sense!" Ashley wanted to scream. Her parents would ruin her chance with Dar. "If you met him, you'd like him."

"That may be so, but the rule stands," her mother insisted.

Pushing back her chair, Ashley stormed to the kitchen doorway. "That is no fair," she shouted. "No fair at all!"

The following day, in school, Ashley told her friends about her conversation with her parents. She walked around the rest of the day in a bad mood, silently fuming.

What a stupid rule! Dar would really think she was a child if she wasn't allowed to go out with him in the evening.

She could just picture it. He'd ask her to the movies and she'd have to say something like, *Sure, as long as we go to the matinee, we're with a group, and my parents drive us.* That would go over *real* big. She'd rather die than say that. She *would* die, in fact—die of total humiliation.

She was thinking these things as she dumped her books into her locker at the end of school. A tap on her shoulder made her jump, causing her to drop several books.

"Oh, um . . . s-sorry, Ashley," Jason Hudson apologized.

"S-sorry." He stooped to pick up the fallen books and handed them back to her.

"That's okay," she said, recovering from her surprise. "I guess I was in another world."

"You—you looked it," he commented. She noticed now that he wore new glasses. She hadn't noticed them earlier in the day. They had chrome wire frames and looked much better on him than the old ones had. *Much better.*

"What's up?" she asked him, shutting her locker.

"I . . . I . . . wanted to ask you s-something."

Alarms went off in Ashley's brain. Was he about to ask her for a date? She hoped not. Ashley suddenly wondered if Molly had been right. Had all her friendliness given Jason the wrong idea?

"Wh-what d-do you kn-know about the P-Pine Manor Woods?" he asked. "S-since you live right n-next to it, and all."

Inwardly, Ashley sighed with relief. Then questions raced through her mind. The woods? Why was he asking? What did *he* know about the woods?

"Th-the oth-ther day Christina mentioned angels, and I w-wondered about it because . . . because, w-well . . . it's . . . it's important."

Ashley studied him without replying. Did he know about the angel who walked with him? Should she mention it? Was that why he was asking?

"Why do you want to know about angels?" she asked, eager to hear his response.

"Do . . . do . . . you th-think I'm nuts?" Jason asked,

worry clouding his face. "I . . . I . . . know . . . know it s-sounds strange, but . . ." His voice trailed off helplessly as he stared at the floor.

"No, it doesn't," Ashley assured him. "Not to me. Not at all." She decided to speak directly. Something about him made her feel that she could. "Jason, there *are* angels in the woods. I've seen them."

Jason fell back into the lockers, shocked by her words.

"I mean, I'm sure angels are all around," she clarified, "but for some reason you can see them more easily in special places in the woods. Christina thinks the woods has energy spots where spirits pass easily between worlds. I don't know about that. I do know that the bridge is the best place to see them."

"Th-the bridge?" Jason asked excitedly. "Th-then th-there *is* a bridge. Have you s-seen it? Could you . . . could you take me th-there?"

Ashley wasn't sure what to say. She and her friends had decided long ago not to take other people to the bridge. They didn't want the woods trampled by curiosity seekers and turned into some kind of cheap tourist attraction. "How do you know about the bridge?" she asked Jason.

"Mom h-heard about it. Th-that's why she moved . . . moved us to th-the woods."

So he did live in the woods. "Why did you say you lived in town?" she asked boldly.

Jason colored. "It's . . . it's . . . kind of s-strange to live in the w-woods."

She shrugged dismissively. "I knew a real nice family who lived in the woods. You must be in their old house. I think it's the only house in the woods, besides the ruins of the old Pine Manor. Why is your mother looking for angels?"

"She's . . . she's sick. Very s-sick."

"And she wants the angels to help her?" Ashley asked as she finally began to understand.

Jason nodded. "Can you b-bring me to the b-bridge?"

"I suppose so," Ashley agreed.

11

Ashley and Jason talked all the way out to the bus, where they joined Christina. He told them how worried he was about his mother. "Sh-she needs to see . . . to see . . . a doctor, maybe even go to the h-hospital. But she w-won't. Sh-she th-thinks only the angels can h-help her."

"We saw you with an angel," Christina revealed solemnly.

Ashley looked at her sharply, surprised that she'd revealed this fact so plainly. But she was right to tell. Jason should know.

Jason listened in silence as Christina told the whole story of seeing him with the glorious golden angel. His face revealed neither belief nor shock when she mentioned that the angel had probably saved his life. It was simply curious and interested.

"If th-the angels a-are h-here, why aren't th-they h-helping her?" Jason questioned when Christina was done talking. He hung his head. "She just gets w-worse every . . . every day."

Ashley and Christina looked at one another helplessly. "You can ask the angels yourself if you go to the bridge," Christina suggested. "They sometimes work in strange ways, so maybe they are helping but you just can't see it."

"W-would you take m-me?" Jason asked, his eyes pleading and hopeful.

"Of course. But I don't want to go after school," Ashley said. "It was nearly dark by the time we got out of the woods the other day. I don't like being in the woods at night. It's so unbelievably, completely dark. It's easy to get lost. How about the weekend?"

"I couldn't go. Mom and I are going to visit some friends of hers this weekend," Christina said.

"Th-the weekend is all right w-with me. I have . . . I have chores and s-stuff on S-Saturday, though. Could we go on S-Sunday?" Jason requested.

"Okay," Ashley agreed. They decided that Jason would come to her house and they'd go into the woods, to the bridge, together.

The bus drove through downtown and stopped beside the woods. The kids who lived in the housing development on the left side of the road poured out of the bus. Jason got off with them and entered the woods on the right.

"Poor guy," Ashley commented as they watched him disappear behind the trees. "All alone in the woods with a sick mother."

"I think it would be nice to live in the woods," Christina countered. "It would be so quiet and beautiful, with lots of positive energy around you."

"Maybe, but what if you had no friends and your mother was sick, like Jason? It would be awfully lonely," Ashley pointed out.

"I suppose," Christina conceded. "Even though we live away from everyone, we always have each other." She smiled at Ashley. The girls had lived together on the ranch since they were five. They were more like sisters than just friends.

For the rest of the ride home, Ashley thought about Jason and his predicament. She liked him and she felt sorry that he had so much to worry about.

The bus slowed at their stop by the barn. As she and Christina got off the bus, Ashley spotted a battered car idling just inside the gate that led to the ranch. A cloud of smoke billowed up from the exhaust pipe. "Dar," she breathed.

He stepped out of the car when he saw her. Ashley inhaled deeply to calm herself. He looked more handsome than ever with the wind tossing his long hair and his hands jammed into the pockets of a scuffed leather jacket.

"Hi. I've been waiting here for you," he greeted them. Waiting for her! Dar had been sitting in his car *waiting . . . for her!* It seemed too awesome to be true. Yet it *was* true. There he was—every gorgeous inch of him, standing in front of her.

"I know I said I'd call, but I can't stop thinking about you. I had to see you, Ashley. Want to go for a ride?" he asked, smiling just a little.

"Okay," Ashley replied immediately. She couldn't say

no, just couldn't. After he'd sat there waiting for her, thinking about her, how could she?

Christina caught her in a warning glance. "What about your parents and the rule?" she muttered between clenched teeth.

Ashley heard her, but looked away. Why did Christina have to be such a goody-goody about this? Ashley wasn't doing anything wrong or bad. Her parents' rule was stupid. They worried too much, and over nothing! "If you see my mother, tell her I went out after school with a friend," she whispered. "It's not a lie."

Christina let out a long, frustrated sigh as Ashley stepped into Dar's car. "Thanks," Ashley called brightly to Christina.

Christina nodded back sourly. Then she turned and walked slowly up the dirt road toward her house.

"Your friend can come, too," Dar offered, obviously sensing the tension between them.

"No, it's not that she wants to come," Ashley explained, smiling. "She's just a worrier."

"What's she worried about?" Dar asked, making a wide U-turn in the dirt drive and heading back out to the main road.

"Oh, I don't know," Ashley said, brushing the question aside. "It's just in her personality to worry."

"I want to show you something," Dar said, a note of excitement in his voice. They drove away from town for about half an hour. Dar played the rock station on the radio loud, drumming along on his steering wheel. The music made it difficult to talk, but Ashley didn't really mind. Just being near Dar was so thrilling that nothing else mattered.

Dar stopped the car at a quiet spot along the road. "What's wrong?" Ashley asked. There was nothing around. This couldn't be what he wanted to show her.

Without answering, he leaped from the car and went to the passenger side. "Come on," he said, as he opened the door and held out his hand to her. She took it, and he helped her from the car.

Dar didn't let go of Ashley's hand as he led her through a stand of bare maple trees at the side of the road. "Where are we going?" she asked.

"To my favorite place," he replied, charging forward so quickly that she had to run to keep up with him. They came out the other side of the trees onto a stretch of old, abandoned railroad tracks. They followed the rusting tracks across the field of brown, dead winter grass until Dar veered off sharply to the left.

Ashley became aware of a thunderous sound in the distance. Before she could ask Dar what the noise was, she saw.

A foaming, spraying white waterfall—about ten feet across—poured over a rocky ridge, dropping nearly fifty feet to a rushing river below. "It's called Angel's Leap," Dar explained proudly, as if he owned the spot, or had created it.

Stretching onto her toes, Ashley saw the source of the incredible waterfall. It seemed to roar out of a huge, craggy, gray boulder high above them. Ashley realized that the water had to come from an underground river that forced its way up at the boulder and crashed down into the river below. "Nature's really amazing," she commented, truly awed by the sight.

"You're amazing," Dar said. He wrapped his arm around her waist and pulled her close. She looked up at him and he kissed her, ever so gently.

After the kiss, he kept his arm around her. They stood, silently, watching the water cascade into the flowing river. Ashley felt as though she were in a trance. She had fallen under the romantic spell of Dar's sweet kiss, his nearness, and the dramatic intensity of the rushing water.

This would be Dar's favorite place. It proved to Ashley that he was more than just a handsome rock-star guy. He was sensitive. A musician. An artist. Only an artist would think to show someone he liked this special spot. And he must like her a lot to share such a personal place with her.

She put her arm around his waist and snuggled closer. This was love—true, romantic love, just the way she'd always dreamed it would be.

"Ashley," Dar said, still gazing out at the waterfall. "The band has a gig up at Newland this weekend. We'll be staying at my friend Jerry's house. The other guys are bringing their girlfriends. Could you come?"

"I'd have to ask my parents," Ashley admitted.

"Don't they let you go away for the weekend?" he asked.

"Sure they do, all the time," she said quickly, not wanting to give him the idea that her parents might think she was too young to spend the weekend with him. "I know they'll say yes. Yeah, it sounds like fun."

He pulled her more tightly to him. "Great," he said. "Totally great."

12

"**Y**es!" Ashley cried triumphantly as she read the note on the kitchen table. Saved! Her parents had gone to a movie at the mall.

The note instructed her to take a TV dinner from the freezer and microwave it. They'd never know she hadn't come home until after eight-thirty.

They'd be back soon, though. Ashley decided to skip dinner and get to her room so it would look like she'd been doing homework for the last few hours. "Oh, no!" she cried, suddenly realizing she didn't have her school backpack.

She'd probably left it in Dar's car. She knew she hadn't taken it to Jimmy's Diner, where they'd sat talking for hours after leaving Angel's Leap. The time had passed so quickly that Ashley was stunned to find it was dark when they finally left the diner.

The phone rang. It was Katie. "Christina told me you went out with Dar," Katie said excitedly, getting right to the point. "How did it go?"

"It went wonderful," Ashley replied dreamily. "He asked me to go with him and the band to a gig in Newland this weekend."

"You're joking!" Katie gasped. "You're not really thinking of going away with him for the whole weekend, are you?"

"Why not?" Ashley asked cautiously. She *was* thinking of going—was determined to go. She didn't want Katie upsetting her plan.

"You *are* going!" Katie screeched incredulously. "You can't! You hardly know him. Besides, your parents won't let you go."

"I'll find a way," Ashley insisted sullenly.

"Ashley!" Katie exploded. "What are you talking about? It wouldn't be like you to run away or sneak behind your parents' backs. I mean, I know you get in trouble at school sometimes, but that's for funny stuff, jokes and pranks. This is serious."

Ashley turned toward the wall so neither of her brothers would hear her conversation if they came in. "Katie," she whispered. "I don't feel like the old me. Dar is so wonderful. Do you know where we went today? He took me to his favorite place in the world, a beautiful waterfall called Angel's Leap. He wanted *me* to see it, Katie. I'm so in love with him. I feel like a completely different person."

"You *sound* completely different. Are you sure about all this? In love?" Katie said, sounding deeply worried. "Love is pretty serious."

"Yes, love. Real love," Ashley gushed. "I have to find a way to go or I'll die."

"You won't die," Katie disagreed wryly.

"Yes, I will," Ashley protested. "I won't *want* to go on living, at least."

"Oh, that's just plain stupid, Ashley."

"Well, maybe not die, but you know what I mean," Ashley continued. "You have to help me think of a way to go. You're good at stuff like that. You have a writer's imagination. What should I do?"

Katie was silent for a moment or two. "Well, not that I think you should go, but . . . you could say you were sleeping over someone's house. It would have to be Molly or me. Christina's too close by. It's risky, though, since our families talk to one another all the time."

Ashley flattened her back against the wall and silently considered Katie's plan. Where could she say she was?

"Rachel Rodriguez!" she cried, jumping forward, suddenly inspired. "I'll say we have to work on the dance together. Plan stuff. That's believable."

"Would Rachel cover for you for an entire weekend?" Katie questioned.

"I don't know. I'll just have to ask her." She might, Ashley decided. Rachel was a good kid, despite her insanely sunny outlook. She might just do it.

The girls talked more, mostly about Dar. Ashley grew increasingly irritated with Katie's misgivings about the weekend away with him. She tried not to blame Katie, though. After all, Katie had never been in love. She had no idea how it felt. And she didn't know Dar, not the way Ashley did.

Still, she hung up feeling annoyed—and even more

determined. She ran into her room and grabbed her phone book. As Ashley dialed the number, she hoped Rachel would answer. She did.

Ashley quickly explained the plan to Rachel.

"I really don't want to do this, Ashley," Rachel said after Ashley had finished. "I don't like this whole idea."

"But, Rachel, you don't have to *do* anything," Ashley cajoled, trying not to sound absolutely desperate— which she was. "I'll simply tell my parents we'll be planning the dance all weekend at your house. They won't check up. They never do."

"They don't?" Rachel questioned, a note of surprise in her voice.

"No, they trust me. Besides, when I mentioned we were working together, my mother said she's met your mother. Isn't she a nurse at a doctor's or a dentist's office or something?"

"Dr. Kaufman," Rachel replied.

"That's right. Dr. Kaufman is my mother's dentist. My mother likes your mother a lot. That's what she said. So she won't mind me going to your house."

There was a pause in the conversation as Rachel considered this. Ashley hoped Rachel was weakening, so she pressed on. "I could have just told my mother I was going to your house and not told you—and you'd never have known—but I decided it was only right to tell you."

"I'm glad you did," Rachel admitted. "Still . . . why don't you ask your parents if you can go with Dar? Then you wouldn't have to lie."

"Because I know their answer would be no," Ashley

explained. "And I have to go, Rachel. You saw Dar. You know how unbelievable he is."

"He's awfully cute," Rachel agreed. "I told you he liked you. I guess if I were you, I'd really want to go, too. Okay, but leave me a number where I can call you, just in case something goes wrong."

A flame of pure joy jumped up inside Ashley. "Thanks, Rachel. Thanks! Thanks! Thanks! As soon as I get there, I'll call and give you a number. Nothing will go wrong, though. I promise."

"I hope you're right," Rachel said, unconvinced.

"Really, everything will be fine," Ashley assured her. "We can talk more at school tomorrow. Bye."

Ashley hung up the phone and sighed with relief. *Everything is working out perfectly*, she thought as she walked down the hallway.

Going to her neat bedroom with its lacy spread and matching curtains, Ashley threw herself onto the bed. She was more tired than she realized, and it felt good to lie on the soft bed covers.

In minutes, still fully clothed, she lay sprawled across her pillows in a deep sleep, dreaming . . .

Ashley was walking in a field of tall, waving wildflowers. Winter's cold, blasting winds had turned gentle, as though it were early spring, still cool, but mild.

The smell of eucalyptus leaves filled the air. The sky was a fiery sunset blaze of reds and pinks.

Where am I? she wondered, although she

wasn't truly frightened, merely perplexed.

She spied Jason Hudson standing on the other side of the field. He smiled at her but didn't move toward her. Ashley cut through the fragrant wildflowers—purple-blue cornflowers, Indian paintbrush, orange daylilies, delicate white Queen Anne's lace on tall stalks. *Strange,* she thought, *these are summer flowers, not spring.* This strangeness told her she was in a dream, even while she was in it.

When she finally reached Jason, he revealed a bouquet of vivid red wild roses he had hidden behind his back. "These are for you," he said, presenting them to her.

"How beautiful," Ashley murmured, burying her nose in their fragrant petals. She looked up at him and realized he wasn't wearing glasses. "Did you lose your glasses?" she asked, concerned.

"I can see perfectly in dreams," he replied, softly smiling.

"You're not stuttering, either," she noticed.

"In dreams I speak the way I would like to speak," he said. "In dreams my mother isn't sick and you love me."

Over his shoulder, Ashley suddenly saw the beautiful sunlight-drenched angel that had been with Jason on the other days. Then another angel joined him, a smaller female angel in a lovely white gown of Victorian lace. Even her shimmering wings seemed made from gossamer lace.

Before she could say anything, the two angels

lifted Jason, the male angel holding him under the arms and the female effortlessly grasping his ankles.

They tossed him high into the air.

"Oh, no!" Ashley gasped, dropping her bouquet in surprise. Why were they putting Jason in danger?

But Jason was laughing as he spun through the air. As he descended, the angels patted him from beneath, tossing him back up as if he were no heavier than a soap bubble.

Jason's delighted, happy laughter filled the air. His joy was contagious. It made Ashley beam with pleasure to watch him. Without even realizing it, she, too, began laughing, her insides expanding with more happiness than she'd ever felt before.

When Ashley's eyes opened, she was still grinning. Her cheeks even ached slightly from all the smiling.

Her room was dark, and she was under her warm quilt. Wiggling her toes, Ashley realized someone had pulled off her boots. Her mother, most likely. She rolled over and shut her eyes, hoping that if she hurried back to sleep she might reenter her dream, but all she found was the soothing nothingness of dreamless sleep.

In the morning, Ashley awakened feeling charged with energy. She was cheerful and alert at breakfast. On the bus to school, she told Christina her dream.

"A dream of angels is always important," Christina declared solemnly. She believed dreams brought messages and even foretold the future.

"What do you think it means?" Ashley asked.

"That there's more to Jason Hudson than we realize," Christina speculated thoughtfully.

"Could be," Ashley agreed, turning from Christina and gazing out the window at the passing landscape of trees and houses. "But what?"

At school, as she headed for her locker, Ashley spotted Jason coming down the hall. His walk was livelier than usual. His shoulders weren't stooped. He looked happy.

"Hi, Jason." She greeted him when he was near enough. "You seem to be in a good mood today."

He smiled nervously. "Yes . . . yes . . . I am."

"Did something good happen?" she asked, hoping it was so.

"No, n-nothing in particular. Just . . . just . . . a good mood, I guess."

"Oh, well, it's good to be in a good mood," she commented, feeling foolish but not knowing what else to say. Turning to leave, she said, "I'll see you in homeroom."

"Ashley." Jason spoke urgently, as if he didn't want her to go. "W-would you . . . you . . . come to my h-house this afternoon. I'd like you . . . you . . . to t-talk to Mom."

"Okay," Ashley agreed quickly. "But I can't stay long."

"No . . . no problem," Jason assured her, a smile slowly overtaking his entire face. "I've g-got to get t-to my locker. See you in h-h-homeroom."

"Okay. See ya!" Ashley said, and ran off. She wanted to get to her locker and find Rachel before the first bell rang.

13

After school that afternoon, Ashley got off the bus with Jason and followed him through the woods. She saw where she and Christina had lost him the other day. Just before the amazingly beautiful waterfall—Christina's power spot—he'd turned sharply off to the left instead of going down to the falls, as they'd done. Once Ashley and Jason made that left, she had a good idea where he'd be going. He was clearly headed for the house that used to belong to a woman named Karen and her kids. It was on the far side of the Angels Crossing Bridge, very deep into the woods. Ashley had been there before. It was the only house in the woods, at least the only one she knew of, besides the decaying remains of Pine Manor, the once-beautiful mansion after which the woods had been named.

"How did you and your mom find this house?" Ashley asked as they walked along, side by side when possible, other times in single file to leap a fallen tree branch or maneuver over a grouping of moss-slick boulders.

"My . . . my mother met a craftswoman at a fair. She rented th-the house to us," Jason explained, extending his hand to help Ashley over the trunk of a huge toppled pine. His grasp was surprisingly firm and warm. "Th-the woman wanted to try living in t-town for a while. Mom grabbed the house right away because the woman, I th-think her name was . . . was Karen . . ."

"It is," Ashley confirmed. She noticed that he seemed calmer, more at home here in the woods. Even his stammer had lightened.

"Karen told her th-there were angels in the woods. Mom's convinced angels are the . . . the only ones who can cure her." As Jason spoke about this, his shoulders slumped forward. He wore a look of defeat.

"You don't believe in angels?" Ashley inquired.

"It's possible, I guess," he said, raising his head and speaking passionately. "It's just th-that I don't think a person should sit around in the woods waiting for . . . for them to show up and fix everything. Mom should be finding a doctor who can help her. Maybe she sh-should even be in the hospital. I don't know. But I can't s-stand just sitting around waiting for angels. If we can go to the bridge and find th-them, at least it would be better th-than waiting."

"But there's an angel with you," Ashley quietly reminded him. "Don't you remember what Christina said?"

Jason stopped walking and looked deeply into Ashley's eyes. "I know the two of you wouldn't lie to me, but it's p-pretty hard to believe. If an angel is s-so close, why doesn't he do something for Mom? Sh-she just gets paler and thinner every day."

"Do you know what's wrong with her?" Ashley asked gently.

Jason shook his head. "Sh-she went to a doctor who ran some t-t-tests. He couldn't tell anything from those tests so he wanted to run some more. He wanted to check . . . check for cancer, and that scared her, I think."

"Cancer," Ashley echoed in an awed murmur. She knew that the disease was serious, and she understood how it might frighten a person. "But doctors can treat cancer," she said, remembering a television show she's seen about people who had cancer but had gotten better. "There's a lot doctors can do for people with cancer."

"Tell . . . tell . . . her that," Jason pleaded sincerely. "She might listen to you."

They began walking again. "Well, I don't know, Jason. I don't even know your mother. Why would she listen to me? Besides, it's kind of personal. I can't just barge in on a grown-up and start lecturing her about cancer. She might not even have it."

"I don't know what . . . what else to do, Ashley," he said, his voice a choked sob.

Ashley put her hand on his shoulder. "It will be all right. We'll figure something out."

"Thanks, Ashley. I hope you're right."

"Jason!" Ashley said. "Do you realize that you didn't even stammer once just then?" A quick wave of embarrassment swept over her. How could she have been so tactless?

"I know. I'm not stuttering and stammering like an idiot," he said.

"I don't think you're an idiot, but . . . yeah . . . you're not stuttering. Why?"

Jason shrugged. "The farther I walk into the woods, the easier it is for me to talk. I don't know why." He laughed scornfully. "I can talk fine when I get to a place where there's nobody to talk to—except Mom, of course."

"Maybe you're more relaxed here," Ashley ventured. "I know I always feel peaceful when I come here."

"Maybe," Jason agreed. They walked silently onward.

Ashley knew she'd offered a logical explanation for Jason's improved speech, but secretly, she wondered if there was more to it. Was there something magical in the woods that stopped him from stuttering? Ashley had certainly experienced it herself—that feeling of being in a sacred, powerful place. "Look," she said, holding her wrist up to Jason.

He frowned down at her watch, puzzled. "Do you have to head home?" he asked.

"No. Look. It stopped. It always stops here in the woods."

His eyes widened in wonder. "Wow. I don't stutter. Your watch stops. What does it all mean?"

Ashley shrugged and shook her head seriously.

It wasn't long before they came to the house just over the ridge of a hill. The first floor was built of stone. The second story was built of wood with heavy wooden trim. The roof was peaked and then flattened out to a sort of railed observatory deck on top. An amateur stargazer's telescope sat on top of the observatory deck, aimed at the stars.

Ashley remembered how Karen's children always played out on the hilly grass in the treeless clearing around the house. She also remembered how run-down the house had been. Karen must have worked hard to get it ready for Jason and his mother.

They entered the shadowy house, and Ashley was immediately struck by the smell of mildew. "Jason?" a whispery voice called from a room off to the left of the front door. Jason guided Ashley into the cramped living room.

A woman sat in a chair in the corner, wrapped in a throw blanket. As Jason had described, she was painfully thin. Dark shadows surrounded her eyes. Her brittle, nearly colorless hair was pushed back with a black headband.

"This is my friend, Mom. Her name is Ashley," Jason introduced her.

"Nice to meet you," Ashley said shyly. "We're sort of neighbors. I live just on the other side of the woods, at the ranch."

"Do you spend much time in the woods, Ashley?" the woman asked. It seemed as though merely speaking was an effort for her, yet she urgently wanted to ask this question.

"Yes, I—"

"She knew the people who used to live here," Jason cut in anxiously.

"Actually, my friend Christina knew them better than I did, but she brought me here with her sometimes and—"

"Angels," Mrs. Hudson cut her off. "Have you seen angels?"

Ashley's eyes darted to Jason. What should she say? With an almost unnoticeable shake of his head, he signaled her to say no.

"Don't you tell her what to say!" his mother demanded sharply. "Have you seen angels, dear?"

"Yes!" Ashley blurted.

Jason scowled at her. Ashley realized why he didn't want her to say anything. He wanted his mother to get proper medical attention. As long as Ashley held out the hope of angels, Mrs. Hudson wouldn't do anything to help herself.

"But, you know, they're very unpredictable," Ashley added, trying to make it up to Jason. Her words tumbled forth rapidly. "They never do what you think they will. In fact, there's no telling what they'll do, or not do. It's like, they don't think the way we do. Not at all. One time the angels told me they influenced some teenage boys to steal a car so the man who owned it, who was drunk, couldn't get into it and crash. The angels wanted the boys to be caught while they were still underage and would have a chance to change their ways instead of going to jail. Who would ever think angels would do something like that? And another time—"

"You've *talked* to the angels?" Mrs. Hudson asked, her thin, whispering voice rising to a hollow, breaking croak.

The interruption knocked Ashley off track. For a moment, she lost her train of thought. "Yes," she confirmed, nodding.

"How do you contact them?"

"At the bridge," Ashley admitted. Mrs. Hudson was so direct that Ashley couldn't respond any other way. The woman's need to know was so pressing and heartfelt, Ashley had to address it directly.

Mrs. Hudson pushed forward in her seat, propelled by her own excitement. "What bridge?"

"Ashley's going to take me there on Sunday," Jason told her. "But that doesn't mean anything, Mom. You heard her. The angels don't always come, and even if they do, they might not do anything for you. There might not be anything they *can* do."

"Thank you. Thank you," Mrs. Hudson said to Ashley in a whisper, ignoring her son.

Ashley felt caught between Jason and his mother. She wanted to get out of there, to be home, away from this whole unhappy problem. She glanced uneasily at the old clock on the mantel.

"That hasn't worked since we moved here," Jason told her. "Now I know why." He turned toward his mother to explain, but her eyes were closed.

"Mom?" he asked anxiously, his voice shaking nervously.

She nodded but didn't have the strength to open her

eyes. Jason exhaled with relief. "Come on," he said quietly, guiding Ashley out of the room. "You'd better go. You don't want to be caught out here after dark. I'll walk you home."

"You don't have to." Ashley declined the offer. "I'll have enough time to make it, and I know the way from here. Besides, if you walk me home, then it will get dark on your way back and *you'll* get lost."

"Are you sure you'll be okay?"

"Positive."

They walked together outside to the top of the hill where the woods began. "Bye. See you in school," Jason said.

The sweet puppy-dog look on his face told her how sad he was to see her go.

"Bye," Ashley said, waving as she walked away. What a lonely life Jason had. She thought of the activity and laughter in her own sunny, busy house. She compared that to Jason's quiet home life, there, all alone with his sick mother, worried that at any moment she'd fall asleep and never awaken, leaving him entirely alone in the world. The idea of it made a quick, cold chill run down her spine.

In order to get home, Ashley had to go over the Angels Crossing Bridge. She resolved that if she saw any sign of the angels, she'd beg them to do something for Jason and his mother.

As she walked, Ashley wondered about the angel she had seen with Jason. Why didn't he do anything to help? Sure, he stopped Jason from walking into the road. But if he made Jason's mother well, he'd be helping Jason in the best way possible. If she were healthy again, they'd certainly move to someplace less isolated. And if he wasn't constantly worried about his mother's illness, Jason could have a normal life.

"Hello?" she called as she stepped onto the bridge. "Anybody home?"

She wished Christina were with her. Christina was so much more relaxed with the angels, probably because she didn't think it was one bit surprising or strange that people should talk to angels. Ashley, on the other hand, could never get over it. Each time it happened, it was totally amazing to her.

"I have a question," she called out. "It's kind of important. Anybody here?"

She stood, waiting. The creek splashed noisily below. Bare branches snapped and fallen leaves crackled as small animals moved through the woods on either side of the bridge.

No angels.

"Okay," she called, just in case somehow they could hear her. "I'll be back Sunday with a friend of mine. If you could be around . . . please. Like I said, it's important."

Ashley continued on to the other side of the bridge. A small, feathery-light sound behind her made her turn back sharply.

On the top of the roof sat Edwina. Her blond curls waved lightly in the breeze.

She flashed a dazzling smile at Ashley.

Then she was gone.

"Wait!" Ashley cried, stepping forward. At that moment, she realized she was holding something in her right hand. Looking down, she saw it was a piece of paper, a note of some kind.

Slowly, she unfolded it and began to read the words handwritten on the paper.

14

At first, Ashley was so surprised that she couldn't make sense of the words on the page.

Then she realized. It was a poem.

Angel in the Woods

A hint of sun
among the trees.
A glance. A smile.
A sudden breeze.
There's an angel in the woods today.

Shadows lift.
The sun appears.
New day. New hope.
The end of tears.
There's an Ashley in the woods today.

The poem was signed in neat script at the bottom—
Jason Hudson. It was dated, too. He'd written it today!

Unexpectedly, Ashley felt a lump in her throat, as if
sentimental tears were welling inside her. She was so
touched! He'd written this poem about her.

But when?

Was he writing it right now?

With the angels, anything was possible. They jumped
back and forth through time as easily as crossing a
street.

She looked back to the bridge's roof, hoping Edwina
would reappear and explain this. But all she saw were
the lengthening shadows of the trees on the old shingled
roof.

Those growing shadows reminded her to get moving.
Night sneaked in fast this time of year. She'd been lost in
these woods after dark before. It wasn't an experience
she longed to repeat.

Folding the poem into her jacket pocket, Ashley
climbed the steep hill going away from the bridge. As she
walked, questions raced in her head. Why had Edwina
given her this poem? What did the angel want her to
know? That Jason was a poet? How he felt? That the
angels were on the job to help him? That they weren't
going to help him? What?

Mrs. Hudson needed some serious help—that much
Ashley knew for sure. But was it angel help, or doctor
help? Neither kind seemed to be coming her way. If
something didn't happen soon, Jason's mother would
just waste away there in the woods. It was insane!

Ashley emerged from the trees just as the last rays of light disappeared over the back of her house. With the sun down, she was suddenly very cold.

Her golden retriever, Champ, scrambled down the steps to greet her as she approached her front porch. "Hi, fella," she murmured, absently ruffling the soft, rust-colored fur between his ears.

Almost the very moment she entered the house, the phone rang. She let it ring several times, hoping someone else would pick it up. No one seemed to be around, so she grabbed the phone in the kitchen. "Hello?"

"Hi, Ashley, it's Dar."

Dar! Immediately her heart began to race. How she loved the sound of his voice.

"Listen," he said. "What's happening for tomorrow? Are we on?"

Ashley glanced guiltily at the door for any sign of her parents. She turned toward the wall. "It's all set," she told him. "No problem."

"Your parents are cool with you spending the weekend with me?" he asked.

"Oh, yeah. Totally cool," she lied, not wanting to sound like a child whose parents would object to her spending a weekend away.

"Great." He went on to tell her where they'd meet and what time.

"Wait a minute," Ashley said suddenly. "I just thought of something . . ." Oh, no! Jason. She'd promised to go with him to the bridge Sunday. How could she have totally forgotten she'd be away? "What time will we be back on Sunday?"

"I don't know . . . around three."

"Three," she echoed thoughtfully. That would be good enough. She would still have time to go to the bridge with Jason if she got back by three. "That's fine," she assured him. "I'll see you Friday. I can't wait."

15

That Friday, after the final school bell, Ashley pulled her flowered canvas overnight bag from the bottom of her locker. She'd been tormented with guilt for the entire day. When she'd kissed her mother good-bye that morning, she'd felt as though the word *liar* was printed across her forehead.

The awful guilt evaporated the moment she saw Dar pull up to the front of the school in a friend's van. "All set to go, babe?" he asked as she climbed in.

Babe? She wasn't exactly sure how she felt about being called *babe.* In a way, it was nice. The word made it sound as though they were officially boyfriend and girlfriend. Yet, in another way, it was impersonal. He could have called any girl *babe.* It wouldn't have mattered who it was.

She decided not to worry about it. His gorgeous smile told her he was glad to see her, and that was all that mattered.

Seated next to her, Dar slung his arm casually around her shoulders. The other band members were there—Ricky, the drummer; Max, the keyboardist; Greg, the lead guitarist; and Archer, another guitarist. Three girlfriends, Brittany, Sue, and Amanda, were also there. Ashley recognized two of the older girls from the cafeteria practice.

During the hour-long drive, the band members mostly discussed the upcoming performance, going over keys and chords and song lyrics. The girls talked about people they knew in high school. They tried explaining to Ashley who each person was, but Ashley couldn't keep all the names straight.

In little over an hour, they drove into Newland, the home of Newland College. "Party town, USA!" Ricky whooped wildly.

"My brother is a junior at Newland," said Brittany, Ricky's blond girlfriend. "He just goes to one party after another. I am definitely going to school here when I graduate."

"When does he study?" Ashley asked.

"Study!" Dar laughed. "Nobody at Newland studies. They're all either jocks or theater heads."

"What do you mean?" Ashley asked, feeling very young and stupid.

"It means," explained Sue, a lean, burgundy-redhead, "that they're here to play sports—Newland's basketball team is number one in their division—or they're in the drama department and all they care about is becoming famous movie stars."

"The main thing," Archer said, running his hand over his spiky blond buzz cut, "is not to let on we're in high school. A bunch of college kids won't come out to hear some high school kids play. I told the guy who runs the club that we all graduated two years ago." He looked specifically at Dar. "So keep Little Miss Junior High here out of sight."

Ashley's cheeks burned with embarrassment and anger.

"Don't you worry about her, man," Dar snapped. "Ashley's cool. She's not the one who acts like an overgrown kid. Remember who barfed up beer and cookies at our last gig."

"Oh, like you never drank too much," Archer shot back defensively.

"But I didn't eat two bags of chocolate chip cookies on top of it," Dar shot back.

The van stopped in front of a brightly painted Victorian-style house in a row of similarly bright houses. Despite their colorful shingles, the houses all appeared to be rather rundown. "This is your friend's house?" Ashley questioned. It wasn't at all what she'd expected.

"Yeah," he replied, helping her out of the van. "My buddy graduated from Pine Ridge High last year. He goes to college here now and shares this house with a bunch of guys."

"How *many* guys?" Ashley asked as a stream of college kids, girls and guys, went in and out of the front door of the house.

"I don't know," Dar admitted, laughing. "I don't think he even knows. There are always so many people around."

A boy in a football jersey and no coat bumped into Ashley and hurried by without apologizing. "I can see that," Ashley said. "It looks pretty wild."

"Don't worry. It'll be cool," Dar whispered, putting his arm around her waist and guiding her up the stairs and into the house.

Inside, Dar was greeted by his friend, a short, stocky guy named Jerry. "You can crash up in the attic," he said, leading them up narrow wooden stairs. Ashley and the rest of their group followed him up three levels. At the very top he opened the door to a big, open, empty room. Two stained-glass windows on either side let in colorful, muted light. "There are some futons, sleeping bags, pillows, and blankets in the closets," Jerry informed them.

"Awesome!" announced Amanda, a girl with dyed black hair and heavy eyeliner. She was with Archer. "This is great."

Ashley didn't see what was so great about the space. To her it was just an empty room, soon to be awfully crowded. It wasn't what she'd expected *at all*.

"What's the matter?" Dar asked.

"Does it show?" Ashley asked, embarrassed.

"You're not happy about *something*," he said. "I can see it in your face."

Ashley turned toward him, away from the others. "This room. There's no privacy at all. And there are so many people running around the house."

"That's college life at Newland," Dar explained with a casual shrug. "You'll get used to it."

Ashley nodded. Maybe she was being immature. She'd try to adjust. "Come on, babe," Dar said, putting his arm around her. "I think you need to get out of here. Let's go for a walk."

She smiled up at him. "Sounds good." He was so great. With Dar beside her, Ashley was positive it would be a wonderful weekend, despite this crazy house.

16

"Sorry, miss. Without proper identification, I can't let you in," the burly man at the entrance of the club told Ashley.

"But I'm with the band," Ashley protested. "I just want to listen to them."

"Like I said, sorry. It's the law," the man insisted. Turning his attention away from her, he began checking ID's for the other customers entering the club.

Ashley sighed deeply. Dar and the others were already inside. They'd gone in the side entrance. She should have gone in with them when she could. Instead, she'd gone back to the van to get her purse, which she'd forgotten.

She went down the narrow alley that separated the club from another shop and knocked on the metal door the band had used. No one answered. She banged harder, with all her strength. She could hear the twang of guitar strings and the ear-aching sound of the speakers being tested. It was too noisy in there. They'd never hear her.

Hugging herself for warmth, Ashley noticed, for the first time, that it was really cold. The tip of her nose burned with the coldness. Maybe she could go sit in the van and try to warm up.

When she got there, though, it was locked. The quaint shops and galleries on the street all seemed to be closed for the night. Now what was she going to do?

A cloud of steam whipped around her as she sighed with frustration and leaned heavily into the van, folding her arms tightly against the cold. She'd have had a better time if she really were at Rachel's house. Right now she was cold, felt totally out of place, and wished she were anywhere else.

"Feeling blue?" inquired a smooth male voice.

Ashley looked up at the speaker. A tall, gangly young man of about eighteen with scraggly dark blond hair huddled into a faded blue woolen jacket. His large blue eyes seemed to bulge just a little. While he wasn't handsome, his face had a pleasant quality.

"Sort of," Ashley admitted.

The young man stuck his hand out to shake hers. "Gabe Headol. Fellow shutout."

Ashley smiled as she grasped his warm hand in hers. "What do you mean?"

"I'm a drummer without a drum. A band member without a band. A musician in search of music."

"I still don't get it," Ashley admitted.

Gabe leaned against the van beside her. "My band, the Dingalings, broke up. Nobody could agree on anything, not even what songs to sing. I was using the lead singer's drums, but now I don't have those anymore. I'm a drumless drummer, what a bummer."

"Too bad," Ashley sympathized. "What are you doing around here?"

"Just walking around. Thinking."

"What are you thinking about?"

"Not much. I think my brain froze."

"Mine's going to freeze soon," Ashley said. "Is there anyplace open around here? A supermarket or a movie theater?"

Gabe appeared to think hard about this. "Actually . . . no."

"What about the college?" Ashley suggested. "Could we go there?"

"Possibly." His eyes lit. "But I know a better place." He began walking down the street, not even looking to see if she was with him. Ashley had to run every few steps to keep up with his long, loping strides.

As much as she liked Gabe instinctively, Ashley still felt cautious. Should she follow him? He was a stranger, after all. And even though he seemed nice, he was a little odd. She decided she wouldn't leave this main street. Here, it was pretty well lit, and cars passed at regular intervals. If he turned any corners, she wouldn't follow.

"Ta da!" Gabe said, stopping in front of a narrow building. Ashley read the sign on the window. Madame Rosa's Teahouse. Tea Served—Fortunes Told. She scowled skeptically at Gabe. "Is this a fortune-telling place?"

"Madame Rosa is a total fake," he said matter-of-factly. "But she serves great tea."

A frigid blast of wind swept under Ashley's jacket. "Let's go," she agreed with a shiver. Gabe pulled the door open and held it for her.

Inside the tiny shop, six small tables covered with white cloths were jammed together. The soft light from the ceiling lamps fell on the tables and wooden floors in dappled spots. Looking up, Ashley saw that the lampshades were made from metal colanders, the type her mom used to drain the water from spaghetti. The light poured out through the holes in the colander and moved with every small breeze. Thick red velvet drapes lined the front windows.

"Welcome, friends!" A heavy middle-aged woman emerged from the back. There was no doubt that she was Madame Rosa. Her long black hair was swept back in a rainbow-colored scarf. She wore so much jewelry that she jangled with every movement. Her face was heavily made up. "Welcome," she repeated with a strong eastern European accent. She pinched Gabe's cheek. "Hello, my darling. You need tea. It is so cold tonight. You wait. I bring."

They seated themselves at a table. In minutes, Madame Rosa returned with a tray containing a teapot, a bowl of sugar, a small pitcher of milk, two cups, and a basket of muffins. She poured them each a cup of the pungent tea.

"Thanks," Ashley said, pulling off her fleece gloves and wrapping her frozen hands around the soothingly warm cup. She eagerly lifted the steaming brew to her lips.

"Stop!" Madame Rosa cried, "Don't drink that tea!"

Ashley jumped, almost spilling the hot liquid. "Why not?"

Madame Rosa produced a small strainer from a pocket in the folds of her long skirt. She placed the strainer on top of the teapot and poured the tea in Ashley's cup back into the pot. Tiny, black, wet tea leaves remained in the strainer. With a flourish she banged the strainer on the table, where it left a soggy clump of tea leaves.

Astonished by all this, Ashley looked to Gabe for an explanation, but his eyes were locked on Madame Rosa in rapt fascination. She stared at the tea leaves on the table, squinting her dark eyes at them. "I see . . . I see . . . many things. Many things are formed in the picture of the future the tea leaves have created for you alone. I see a bird. That means travel. You will go to many places. I see pyramids behind the bird. Soon you will depart for Egypt."

Madame Rosa peered closer, bending to the tablecloth until her nose almost touched the wet tea leaves. "I see a young man. You will find romance in Egypt and live there forever."

A phone in the back of the shop rang. "Excuse me," Madame Rosa said dramatically and rushed off to answer it, jangling as she departed.

"Wow!" Ashley said, letting out a puff of anxious laughter. "That was pretty wild."

"Any plans to go to Egypt?" Gabe asked.

"No."

"I didn't think so." Gabe spooned four teaspoons of sugar into his tea and sipped it. "What picture do you see in the leaves?" he asked.

The question surprised Ashley. "Should I see a picture?"

"Look," he suggested. "You never know."

Ashley studied the mess of soggy tea leaves on the table. To her surprise, she did see shapes in the leaves. "I think I can see an angel," she murmured, studying one spot. It was probably what Madame Rosa had called a bird, but, though it seemed to be a winged creature, to Ashley it very definitely had a human shape with wings.

"An angel, eh," Gabe repeated, looking on with interest.

"I see the guy Madame Rosa saw, too." Ashley pointed to the place where the leaves seemed to form a boy.

"Any idea who it is?" Gabe asked.

"I don't know," Ashley said. "I can't see him clearly enough."

Madame Rosa returned with a fresh cup for Ashley. "You'll like Egypt," she said as she poured. "Much warmer there than here. This weather, oh, it's the worst. My bones ache all the time."

"Yes, I'm sure I'll like it," Ashley replied, looking at Gabe with laughing eyes.

"Say hello to the Sphinx for me," Gabe joked.

Ashley smiled back at him. This evening was turning out so much better than she'd expected.

17

"This is a disaster! A disaster!" Dar said loudly the next morning, waking Ashley. Sleepily, she lifted her head from the orange beanbag chair where she'd curled up to fall asleep before the band even returned from their job the night before. Now, everyone else was asleep on the floor, on mattresses, on futons, and in sleeping bags, all over the room. Only Dar was awake and dressed, pacing the room.

After their tea at Madame Rosa's, Gabe had phoned a car service to drive Ashley back to the house. He'd written the directions on the back of Madame Rosa's business card.

"What's a disaster?" Ashley asked groggily.

"Ricky, he's sick. He spiked this fever in the middle of the gig last night . . . like . . . from out of nowhere. Now what are we going to do? We're booked for tonight and we have no drummer." As Dar spoke, he clutched at his hair, beside himself with anxiety.

"Can't you play without a drummer?" Ashley suggested, sitting forward.

"No," Dar snapped unpleasantly.

Ashley recoiled silently. He didn't need to be so rude. But he was upset, so she let it pass. Then another distressing thought hit her. "Hey, didn't you notice I wasn't there last night?" she asked, feeling hurt.

Dar stared at her blankly at first. "Oh, yeah . . . yeah. Sorry. I was worried. Where did you go?"

Ashley explained how she was shut out of the club. "At first I thought I might freeze," she told him, "but it worked out all right because I met this guy and—" She cut herself short as an idea came to her. "He's a drummer!" she cried, getting to her knees. "And he was looking for a band to play with."

"No kidding?" Dar said excitedly. "Who is he? What's his name? Is he any good?"

"I don't know," Ashley answered glumly, dropping back into the beanbag chair. "I mean, I know his name, but that's all." As she spoke, her eyes lit on Madame Rosa's card lying on the floor. She picked it up. Madame Rosa seemed to know Gabe, maybe she knew where he lived. Ashley turned the card in her hand. On the front was the name and address of Madame Rosa's tea house. On the back were the directions Gabe had written for the cab driver. At the bottom of the directions he'd added, *Gabe Headol, drummer guy, 264-3500.* "Dar! Here's his phone number."

Dar plucked the card from her hands. "Way to go, babe!" he exulted as he headed for a chipped white phone on the paneled wall by the door. "I hope this guy can play."

Within the next forty-five minutes, Gabe showed up at the house. Ashley was amazed at how glad she was to see him, as if he were a friend she'd known all her life instead of a stranger she'd met in the cold only the night before.

"Why aren't you packing for Egypt?" Gabe teased when he saw Ashley.

"I'm stuck here till tomorrow morning," she replied, laughing.

Impatiently, Dar took Gabe's arm and whisked him off to a corner of the room by the window, where he questioned him about his drumming experience. Gabe answered him in his laid-back, slightly spacy way.

Ashley watched the two of them, framed by the colored glass in the tall window. She could see from his narrow-eyed expression that Dar was wary of Gabe. In a way, Gabe did seem flaky, she supposed. But couldn't Dar see how sweet he was?

Dar was still skeptical after their conversation, but he gave Gabe the job of drumming with the band for that night. He stayed the entire day to work with the other musicians and learn their songs.

Gabe drummed with a professionalism and passion that astounded everyone. The band members, especially Dar, were thrilled with their new find. Ricky stayed on his mattress, jealously scowling at the new drummer, but he was too sick to do anything other than lie there burning with fever.

The girls were friendlier to Ashley, wanting to know where she'd found Gabe. When she told them, they all wanted to go to Madame Rosa's. "I'll make sure you get into the club tonight," Amanda assured her knowingly. "Just stick with me. You should be with Dar. There was a girl in the audience—a college girl—and she was flirting outrageously with him last night."

"She was?" Ashley said, feeling sickened at the idea.

Amanda nodded. "You should be there tonight. Take it from me."

By six that evening, everyone was ready for a pizza break. Ricky snored loudly, wrapped in a sleeping bag, as they stepped over him on their way to the van. Ashley was about to walk out of the room when Dar grabbed her wrist. "We'll meet you there," he called to Archer. "Don't wait."

Ashley looked at Dar questioningly. He pulled her tightly to him as Archer shut the door. "I wanted some time alone with you," he said, his voice low, almost half-teasing.

She smiled at him but didn't feel comfortable. There was something in his voice and expression that made her uneasy.

He kissed her. But this time she didn't like it. She felt her back stiffen.

What was it? She wasn't sure. She hadn't felt this way when he kissed her by the Angel's Leap waterfall. That had been so wonderfully romantic.

Maybe it was the way he was holding her. Too tightly, as though she couldn't pull away if she wanted to.

He kissed her again, this time working his lips down to her neck. His hand slipped under her sweater, touching her skin.

Without thinking, Ashley pushed him away roughly.

"What?" he asked, insulted.

Ashley opened her mouth, but no words came out. She didn't know how to explain, but she didn't like the feeling his touch was giving her. It was like she was being overpowered by an impersonal force. "Maybe . . . maybe . . . I'm not ready . . ."

"For what?" he demanded gruffly.

"For . . ." She couldn't find words to express the feelings she didn't understand herself.

The door swung open. Ashley turned sharply to see Gabe standing in the doorway wearing his pleasant, slightly goofy grin. "You guys coming?" he inquired, seeming not to notice the tension between them. "I told Archer not to leave until I checked. I wouldn't want you to be stranded here without pizza."

Dar stormed across the room, snapping up his jacket from the floor as he went. "Yeah, we're coming." He shoved Gabe slightly as he went out the door.

Unperturbed, Gabe smiled invitingly at Ashley. "Ready to go?"

"Yes," she replied, relieved and grateful to him for interrupting. Had his return been lucky coincidence, or had he guessed there might be a problem? She felt too awkward about it to ask.

At the pizzeria in town, Dar was sullen and moody. Ashley tried to catch his eye, to pry a smile from him, but he wouldn't cooperate. He was just as quiet during the ride back to Jerry's house.

That evening, as they got ready to go to the club, Ashley worried. Had she driven Dar away? Did he think she was a child? Did he hate her now? She applied more makeup than she usually wore, wanting to look more attractive, and older. "You look cool," Amanda told her, coming into the cramped bathroom. She held up her own bag of makeup. "Try this lipstick." She applied a heavy coat of deep burgundy lip color to Ashley's lips. "And some eyeliner would be good," she said, producing a thin black liner pencil from her bag.

When Amanda was done, Ashley turned and stared at her own image in the mirror. She looked so different. Amanda lifted the dark green headband Ashley wore and pushed some of Ashley's front curls into her face. "Now you look totally wild," she pronounced proudly. "Very cool."

Ashley smiled weakly. "Thanks." She reminded herself of the way she'd looked when she played a vampire in the seventh grade Halloween show. But if Amanda said she looked cool, Ashley decided she probably did.

As Ashley came out of the bathroom, she ran into Gabe. He stood in the hallway reading over some music. "So, what do you think of the Newland rock scene?" he asked, looking up from his music.

"It's okay, I guess. I'm looking forward to seeing the show."

Gabe nodded. "I guess your friends at home will want to hear all about it."

"My friends!" Ashley gasped. She'd forgotten to call Rachel with the phone number when she'd arrived yesterday. Hurrying to the wall phone, she quickly punched in the number.

Luckily, Rachel picked up. "Everything's fine at this end," she reported. "How are you?"

"Okay," Ashley replied. "It's a little weird."

"Weird? How?" Rachel inquired, sounding concerned.

Ashley was surprised at how happy she was to be talking to a friendly voice. She told Rachel how everyone was so much older, and what had happened with Dar.

"It sounds like you're in over your head," her friend observed levelly. "Why don't you just come home? You can spend the night at my place for real."

"I can't," Ashley declined. "I have no ride until tomorrow. Besides, Dar would really think I'm a child if I ran out. He's barely speaking to me as it is."

"Forget about him then," Rachel advised. "The world's full of great guys."

Good old optimistic Rachel. "Not guys like Dar," Ashley disagreed. She gave Jerry's number to her friend. "I'll call you tomorrow when I get home."

"Okay. Good luck," Rachel said. "Bye."

That night, in the alley, Amanda handed Ashley a tambourine. "Here, hold this," she advised. "It will make you look like you belong with the band." She tucked Ashley under her arm and pretended to be deep in conversation with her as they shuffled in the side door with the other band members. "There, you're in," she exclaimed as the door closed behind them.

"Thanks." Ashley gazed around at the cramped backstage area. Out onstage, the band began setting up equipment. It was thrilling. For the first time since arriving, she felt like she belonged with the group.

Maybe feeling like an outsider was what had made her act so strange with Dar. She was suddenly desperate to make up with him. She'd try to relax, to be more grown-up. She had to find him, to tell him she was sorry for the way she'd acted.

But where was he? "Have you seen Dar?" she asked Brittany, who was standing nearby.

Brittany shot Amanda a distressed glance.

"Where is he?" Ashley asked urgently.

With a quick jerk of her head, Brittany indicated the black velvet curtain hanging at the corner of the stage. Ashley furrowed her brow in confusion. She didn't see Dar.

"Oh, no, not her again," Amanda grumbled.

"Who?" Ashley asked, still confused.

"That girl from last night. The one I told you to watch out for," Amanda growled, glaring at the curtain.

That was when the curtain moved, sweeping away from the two figures it had been covering. Ashley saw what Amanda and Brittany had seen first.

Dar was standing there kissing a slim girl with long blond hair.

With a clatter, Ashley dropped the tambourine to the floor as her hands flew to her cheeks in horrified surprise. Hot tears jumped to her eyes. No! She didn't want to cry. Not there, not in front of everyone.

Alerted by the crashing tambourine, Dar turned his head and faced his audience. For a moment, his eyes met Ashley's. There was no embarrassment or apology in his expression. His look was so blank, it was almost as if he'd shrugged his shoulders and said, "Well, what did you expect?"

Blinded by tears, Ashley groped for the door, plunging out into the cold alleyway.

18

Ashley sat with her chin pressed against the windowsill as she stared out at the passing cars. She'd taken the car service back to the house, desperate to get as far away from the club as possible.

She'd sat in the dimly lit empty room for two hours hoping that each car that passed would stop in front of the house and that Dar would jump out and bound up the front steps. He'd beg her forgiveness. He'd say he only kissed that girl to make her jealous.

Downstairs, the sounds of a wild party wafted up through the floorboards. On her way up the stairs, a girl had invited Ashley into the second-floor room to join in, but she'd declined. Through the open door she'd seen Ricky, wrapped in a throw blanket. Apparently he was well enough to go to the party. He had waved to her listlessly and she'd waved back, but she was in no mood to be with people, especially not strangers at a party.

She dropped her head on her arms and let her tears

spill out uncontrollably, soaking her sleeve. There was no need to hide them now. No one was there to see. Black eyeliner streaked the front of her sweater. *I must look a mess*, she thought. Who cared? She was all alone.

She thought of home, of her friends, of the woods and the bridge. How she wished she were near the bridge now. She needed the angels' advice and love. Closing her eyes, she pictured herself there. "I don't know what's important anymore," she whispered, as though she were on the bridge talking to the angels. "I don't know what to do. What's right? Please help me think clearly. I'm all mixed up."

She dropped her head again and drifted into a light sleep. After a half hour or so, she awakened and felt a desperate need to talk to someone who cared about her. She went to the wall phone and called Christina. After a ring and a strange beep, a recorded voice came through the receiver. "Service has been interrupted on this line," the recorded voice said in a flat, unemotional tone. "Until further notice this line will receive only incoming calls."

"They didn't pay the bill," Ashley mumbled, glumly returning the receiver to the hook. She must have caught Rachel today just before the phone company turned off half the service. She knew this because it had happened for one day at the ranch when her parents were having money problems.

The door opened with a slight creak. Ashley whirled toward the sound, praying Dar would walk into the room.

"Hi," Gabe greeted her quietly.

Ashley looked around him. "Where's everyone?"

"Went to some party across town," he replied. "I came here to see how you were."

Ashley's heart leaped with gratitude. Someone *did* care about her. The horrible lonely ache in her heart suddenly hurt much less. "How did the show go?" she asked quietly.

Gabe shrugged. "They're not such a hot band," he commented casually. He perched against the windowsill. "Their music is simple and their lyrics are, well . . . simpleminded."

"Do you really think so?" Ashley asked, crossing the room to him. It somehow pleased her to hear him knock the band off their pedestal. She realized she was tired of adoring Dar and his friends. It was a relief to know that other people didn't think they were so great.

"They need words with some real meaning to them," Gabe continued, tapping his heart. "Ones that come from inside." Reaching into his pocket, he pulled out a tattered sheet of paper. "Something like this," he said, holding out the paper to her.

Ashley took it and began to read. It was Jason's poem, "Angel in the Woods." "Where did you get this?" she murmured, in shock.

"I found it blowing around in the alley," he replied. "Now this guy's a real poet. A little rough yet, maybe, but he's got some real feeling here. This could even be a song lyric. Too bad he dropped his poem."

"I dropped it," Ashley confessed. "I forgot it was in my pocket."

Gabe appeared surprised. "You did? Well, you shouldn't forget stuff like that. It's important. He sounds like a nice guy."

"He is," Ashley agreed. "He's had a rough life, though."

"Great things come from people who survive rough lives," Gabe commented. "This guy could grow up to be a great writer if he keeps trying."

"Jason?" Ashley questioned.

"Sure. It sounds like he's already on his way. I'll bet he's a good friend, too."

Ashley nodded in agreement. It would be good to see Jason tomorrow, she realized. She could be herself with him. Thinking about the next day made her realize how late it had grown, and how tired she felt. She yawned. "Sorry," she apologized to Gabe. "It's not the company."

"You'd better get some sleep," Gabe advised, heading for the door.

"Thanks for coming by," Ashley said sincerely. "Will you be around tomorrow before we leave?"

Gabe smiled gently. "I'm always around."

Early Sunday morning, Ashley was awakened by a hand shaking her shoulder. "Wake up," Amanda urged her. She appeared half asleep, her makeup smeared across her face. "There's a phone call for you. The girl says it's urgent."

Ashley sprang forward in the beanbag chair, instantly awake. "Who is it?"

"I don't know, but she sounded upset."

Dashing around the sleepers strewn across the room,

Ashley noticed Dar wasn't there. Had he stayed over at the party? Still wondering where he was, she snapped up the phone dangling from its coiled wire. "Hello?"

"Ashley, thank goodness. It's Rachel. Your mother just called looking for you."

Ashley's heart pounded painfully against her breastbone, all her concerns about Dar forgotten. "Oh, no! What did you say?"

"That you were in the shower. She expects you to call her back, though. She apologized for calling so early but she said it was important that she talk to you."

Important? What could she want? Ashley wondered frantically. Was something wrong at the ranch? Was someone sick, or hurt? Her mind raced with all the horrible possibilities. "Thanks for calling, Rachel. I'll phone her from here."

"Let me know what happens," Rachel requested.

"All right," Ashley promised. "I'm going to hang up now so I can call."

"Okay. Bye." With a click, Rachel hung up. Ashley stood beside the phone a moment, trying to calm her thundering heart. *This is no biggie,* she told herself. *I'll call and see what's going on. It's probably nothing.*

She hoped it was nothing. The band had been out late and they probably wouldn't rouse themselves until at least noon. It would take over an hour to get home. There was no way she could get there fast if she was needed.

She'd just have to hope for the best.

She picked up the receiver and called her home

number. *Stay calm*, she urged herself as she listened to it ring.

The ringing stopped and a beep sounded. "Service has been interrupted on this line. Until further notice, this line will receive only incoming calls," said the flat, uncaring voice from the phone company.

19

Ashley hugged herself tightly to keep out the cold as she did an anxious jig on the curb outside the small country store. The man on the pay phone was taking his time. It seemed he'd been talking to the person on the other end forever.

It had taken Ashley close to twenty minutes to walk to this pay phone. Had her mother called Rachel back looking for her in the meantime?

Finally, the man hung up and walked away from the phone. Ashley rushed to it. She pumped several quarters into the slot and dialed her number. "Mom, it's me," Ashley said the moment her mother picked up. "Rachel said you called while I was in the shower. What's up?" She worked hard to keep her voice steady, casual.

"Ashley, do you feel well?" her mother inquired. "You sound odd."

"Ummm . . ." So much for trying to fool her mother. "I didn't sleep well last night," she tried for a half truth.

"You know, sleeping in a strange place and all."

"A boy named Jason Hudson called several times. He said you two made plans today or something. I told him you were at Rachel's, but he's called three times already this morning. He seems extremely eager to reach you. I said you'd call him."

"Did he leave a number?"

"No. Sorry, I assumed you had it."

"That's all right. I'll call information."

"I'll come pick you up at Rachel's if you want," Mrs. Kingsley offered.

"No!" Ashley said too forcefully. "I mean, that's okay. Rachel and I still have some things to go over. I'll call Jason and get things straight with him. Thanks for the call."

"All right, hon. Are you sure you're okay?"

"Fine. Bye, Mom." She felt like such a sneak, lying to her mother like that. Jason must think she forgot him. She should have set up an exact time and place with him before she left, but she'd been so excited about this weekend she hadn't been thinking clearly. Her hopes had been so high, and everything had gone so terribly wrong.

Ashley called information. There was no listing for anyone named Hudson in the Pine Ridge area. She didn't know Karen's last name, the woman who'd lived there before. None of her friends would know Jason's phone number.

There was only one thing left to do. She'd have to hurry back to the house and get everyone moving. The sooner she got home, the sooner she could smooth everything out.

Fat snow flurries drifted from the gray sky. Pulling up her hood, Ashley headed back toward the house, walking with a quick, determined step. Nothing but getting home mattered now.

She caught a glimpse of herself in the window of a parked car. "Ew," she grimaced. Her makeup was smeared, her hair snarled. Her eyes wore a puffed, heavy look caused by sleeplessness and crying. She did *not* look like a girl who'd had a fabulous weekend with the guy of her dreams. Every inch of her now longed to be home in clean clothes with her face washed and her hair combed—Ashley, herself, once again.

Soon, she assured herself. After fifteen minutes, she came to a corner she didn't recognize. The bright Victorian-style houses all looked so much alike. Had she taken a wrong turn somewhere? Apparently, she had. She had no idea where she was.

It was so early that no one was out on the street. Deciding to backtrack, she turned and headed in the direction she'd come from.

The candy-colored houses suddenly seemed to have become a sinister maze of sameness. How would she ever find her way? She felt as though she were walking in circles for close to an hour before, in desperation, she walked up to a house and rang the bell.

A sleepy-eyed college girl answered. Ashley explained that she was looking for Jerry's house. Luckily, the girl knew Jerry and told Ashley how to get back to the house. Ironically, she was only a little over five minutes away. As she ran up onto the front porch, she noticed that the band's van wasn't parked in front. She yanked on the front door, but it was locked. Finally, she rang the bell. After what seemed like a long time, Dar's friend, Jerry, answered. "How come you didn't go with the others?" her asked, scratching his head groggily.

"What do you mean?" Ashley asked as she fought down panic.

"Ricky was feeling worse. He probably shouldn't have gone to the party last night. Anyway, he wanted to get home so they packed up early and left."

"They left?" Ashley cried, aghast. "They left without me?"

"Guess so," Jerry confirmed.

20

"What do you mean, canceled?" Ashley cried to the man behind the ticket window. The Newland train station was nearly empty—just one man sat on a wooden bench with a newspaper in front of him—but there had to be trains going out. There just had to be!

"Sorry, miss," the balding man apologized. "You can see the snow, can't you?"

Turning, she looked out the plate-glass window. White flakes whirled in front of closed brick stores. It was like a scene within a glass snow dome. She'd been so determined to get to the train station as she ran from Jerry's house that she hadn't been totally aware of how heavily the snow was falling.

"The tracks just freeze up in the spots where that line crosses the river on its way to Pine Ridge," the man added. "It's not safe. If you want, you can wait here in the station. There might be a train through in a few hours if it lets up some."

"A few hours," Ashley murmured, hanging her head in defeat. "All right. I'll wait." What choice did she have? She had nowhere else to go.

Jason will simply have to understand, she thought as she threw herself down despairingly on a worn wooden bench against the station wall. But what if he really needed her? He must need her, otherwise he wouldn't have been calling her house so often. He was a shy kid. He wouldn't pester her family if it wasn't important.

Oh, why had she come on this stupid trip? She'd lied to her family. She'd put Rachel in an awkward position. And now she'd let Jason down. She'd betrayed people who really cared about her for someone—Dar—who didn't really care about her at all.

"Stupid, stupid, stupid!" she berated herself in a whisper, staring down forlornly at her own wet boots. As she stared, another pair of scruffy boots came alongside her. She looked up and gasped. "Gabe!"

He smiled his goofy grin. "We seem to meet everywhere." He plunked down beside her and pushed back his disheveled hair. "What's up?"

In a torrent of rushing words, Ashley told him about Jason and all that she'd been thinking, and how she was stuck now and wished she could get back to Pine Ridge more than anything else in the world.

He scratched his chin thoughtfully. "If you could instantly be somewhere else, where would you be right now?"

Ashley smiled ruefully. "That can't happen."

"If it could," he pressed.

"I'd be in front of Jason's house in the woods," she answered without a moment's hesitation. "I guess I feel the worst about letting him down. I can deal with getting caught by my parents and getting into trouble. I deserve that. But hurting Jason's feelings is what makes me feel most terrible."

"It sounds like he's really counting on you," Gabe agreed. "Ashley, do you trust me?"

"Sure, why shouldn't I?" she asked. He'd been nothing but nice to her. Every instinct she had told her he was trustworthy.

He put his hands over her eyes. "What are you doing?" she asked.

"I've never tried this before, but I'm pretty sure it will work," Gabe said to himself. "I read about it in the manual last night."

"What man—" Before she could finish her question, Gabe jabbed her sharply in the right shoulder while he kept his other hand over her eyes. A tingling rush shot up her legs, like pins and needles. The sensation spread up her torso, back down her legs, then up to her neck before it swept across her face. It was a strange, but pleasant, feeling.

And then she was very cold. Freezing.

Gabe's hand was no longer over her eyes. He was gone, in fact.

"My gosh," Ashley whispered as she slowly opened her eyes. She was standing in the woods, right in front of Jason's house.

How had Gabe done that? Who was he anyway? Could he be . . . an angel?

She turned to see Jason looking out the front door. He didn't see her. But his face was anxious and searching. Was he looking for her?

Their eyes met. "Ashley!" he cried, surprised. A smile slowly swept across his face. "Ashley. Wow!" He rushed out the door. "I didn't even see you walk up."

"I . . . I . . . came up the side way," she said. "I didn't mean to startle you."

Jason's smile quickly faded. "I was sorry to bug your mother, but we have to get to the bridge. It's Mom. She can barely move. I don't know what else to do."

"Did you call a doctor?"

Jason shook his head. "I don't know who to call, and Mom told me not to send for an ambulance. She said she won't go to the hospital."

"That's crazy!" Ashley cried. "No offense to your mother, but . . . it is . . ."

"I know," Jason admitted. "You have to take me to the bridge. The angels are the only ones who can help her now."

Ashley wasn't sure how she'd gotten here, but she knew she was here for a reason. She had to be. Angels didn't do anything without an excellent reason.

She grabbed Jason's hand. "Come on." Together, they ran through the falling snow, up the hill away from his house. They ran over logs and through the pines until they came to the creek. They followed its winding path to the bridge.

Their bounding footsteps echoed on the old wooden boards. "Hello?" Ashley shouted. "We need help. Is anyone here?"

They waited.

"We need help!" Jason called boldly. "Please!"

Wind swept through the opening in the bridge. The creek moved along noisily below and beside them.

"They're not here," Jason said glumly after they had waited five minutes.

"They're here," Ashley replied confidently.

"How can you tell?"

"I'll explain some other time." She knew because Gabe had gotten her here. He wouldn't bring her here just to abandon her.

Would he?

Maybe he would, Ashley thought. You could never tell with angels. Maybe he'd brought her this far and now it was up to her.

Yes. That sounded right. It seemed like it might be the answer. She grasped Jason's arm. "We have to get your mother to a hospital. We can't stand here waiting for the angels."

He nodded slowly. "I know." Without further discussion, they ran from the bridge back to his house.

Bursting in the front door, Ashley went right to the phone and called the information line. "I need the emergency room number of the Pine Ridge Hospital, please," she requested.

Jason ran upstairs and bounded back down in a moment, pale-faced. "She's not moving. I can't wake her."

"Is she breathing?" Ashley asked, holding the phone to her shoulder.

Jason nodded. "But she's really pale."

Ashley had reached the emergency room. She told the

person on the other end what was going on. "Okay . . . okay."

"What?" Jason demanded as Ashley hung up.

"The woman said they'll send an ambulance to the ranch, but they can't get into the woods. They'll have to send paramedics out on foot with a stretcher," she reported quickly.

Ashley phoned her house. Jeremy answered and she told him what was happening. "Mom and Dad went out," he told her. "I'm the only one here."

She wished her parents were home. They would know what to do. "Watch for the ambulance," she instructed Jeremy. "It should be there in a few minutes. Could you help them through the woods?"

"I don't know where you are," Jeremy protested. "I only know the horse trails."

Ashley tried to direct him from one of the trails, but when she hung the phone up, she wasn't confident he understood. "What if they don't get here in time?" Jason fretted, pacing across the kitchen floor. "What if she's in a coma?"

"A coma?" Ashley echoed. She knew that was serious. A person could lapse into a deep, sleeplike state. The person might or might not ever awaken.

"She'll be all right," Ashley said, forcing herself to be positive. It wouldn't help now to think the worst. "We've done all we can," she said. "We just have to wait and hope."

Jason flung himself into a kitchen chair and buried his head in his hands. "I can't!" he moaned.

She knelt beside him and rubbed his quivering shoulders. "Yes, you can. We're going to wait and hope together. You're not alone, Jason."

21

The waiting was a torture. "They're lost in the woods," Jason said with grim certainty after nearly forty-five minutes.

Ashley was inclined to agree. It shouldn't have taken this long. "I'll check your mother," she offered, heading for the stairs.

Mrs. Hudson lay in her shadowy room, white and unmoving. Ashley froze in the doorway. Was she . . . dead? She forced herself to move closer. No. She was still breathing.

Ashley shut her eyes. "We need help. Please."

Then, like a direct answer, Ashley heard the sound of beating wings. Her eyes snapped open wide.

Angels?

Jason burst excitedly into the room. "There's a hospital helicopter hovering over the house! But I don't think they can land."

A booming male voice filled the air. "Can you bring the

patient onto the roof? We need the patient on the roof."

Jason and Ashley looked at one another with panicked eyes. How could they manage that?

"There's a small flat space on the roof," Jason suddenly recalled, "and a stairway up to it, like a little observation station. We could try."

With a nod, Ashley began tucking Mrs. Hudson's blankets under her. She was a small, frail woman, yet it wasn't easy to lift her limp body.

The sound of helicopter blades was deafening as they struggled to carry her down the hall. Jason opened a closetlike door, revealing a rickety wooden stairway within. The stairs were like a ladder, going straight up without a slant.

Ashley gazed at it despairingly. They'd never be able to do it.

As she thought this, she realized Mrs. Hudson had suddenly become incredibly light, almost floating. From Jason's startled expression, she could see he was aware of the change, too.

There was no time to spare. "Let's go," Ashley urged.

Jason and Ashley climbed slowly, pushing Jason's mother up over their heads. The frail woman rose with an unnatural smoothness. Someone—some invisible someone—was lifting her from above. There was no other explanation. Alone, Ashley and Jason could never have done it.

The roof hatch was opened by a man in a white medical outfit. He grabbed Mrs. Hudson under the waist and lifted her the rest of the way.

Ashley fought to steady herself on the roof. The wind whipped up by the helicopter blades was nearly overwhelming. The helicopter hovered just about twelve feet above the roof, a stretcher and ladder hanging from its side.

The man and woman medics on the roof worked with rapid expertise to strap Mrs. Hudson to the stretcher attached to the helicopter. "Oh, wow!" Jason gasped as the male medic signaled the pilot to lift the stretcher. His mother hung there in midair a moment as the snow sailed around her. Ashley understood Jason's fear. The stretcher looked so fragile, as if it might be swept off into the wind and snow at any moment.

The woman medic jumped onto the ladder beside the stretcher and steadied it as it climbed through the air. When they were safely on board, the ladder was thrown down again. "I can take one of you," the man told them.

"He's her son," Ashley said. "Go on, Jason."

Jason nodded as the man strapped him to the ladder and then got on behind him. Slowly, they were drawn up into the helicopter. "I'll meet you at the hospital!" Ashley called, waving from the roof.

The helicopter banked slightly to one side and headed up into the sky. As it lifted, Ashley drew in a sharp, shocked breath.

Riding atop the helicopter was the large golden angel she'd seen with Jason before. His long robes flapped violently in the wind of the retreating helicopter. She knew he'd been with them all along.

When the helicopter was out of sight, Ashley returned to the house. On her way downstairs, she looked into Mrs. Hudson's room.

A glowing white form hovered near the bed, appearing to make it, tenderly smoothing the sheets.

She was the lacy white-robed angel Ashley had seen in her dream.

The angel lifted her lavender-blue eyes to Ashley in a warm, visual embrace. Then she faded from view.

22

As Ashley ran through the snowy woods, hurrying toward home, she saw gray figures wandering aimlessly among the ancient pine trees. She immediately recognized Jeremy, who looked hopelessly lost. "Here!" she shouted, racing toward them.

Jason had been right. In the shadowy woods, Jeremy and the medics had lost their way. "But we didn't order a helicopter," one medic said when Ashley told them that Mrs. Hudson was on her way to the hospital.

"Thank goodness someone did," his companion commented.

Ashley led them back to the ranch. "We'll take you to the hospital," the medic offered.

"Tell Mom and Dad where I am," Ashley said to Jeremy. "I'll call when I know what's going on."

The medic gave Ashley a hand up into the waiting ambulance.

The ambulance sped through the streets toward Pine

Ridge Hospital and let her off at the emergency room entrance. "Thanks," Ashley said, climbing out of the back.

"You're welcome," replied a strangely familiar voice.

Looking up sharply, Ashley saw that the ambulance driver was . . . "Gabe!" she gasped. Why hadn't she noticed him before? He had changed his appearance, Ashley realized.

He smiled that dear lopsided smile. "You were great up there, kiddo," he praised her. He waved, a small, clipped wave, and drove off. "I'll be seeing you," he shouted through his open window.

Stunned, Ashley watched the ambulance round the corner of the hospital.

A blast of cold wind swept through her hair and brought her back to reality. She had to go in and find Jason.

The moment she entered the warm emergency room, she saw the commotion. The paramedics were rushing Mrs. Hudson away through swinging doors.

"Ashley," Jason cried, hurrying to her. "It's her heart. They're going to operate. They said they don't have one minute to wait."

He gripped her hand tightly. Ashley squeezed his in return. She noticed he wasn't stuttering. His concern for his mother must have made him forget his self-consciousness. Or maybe the calmness of the woods had become part of him now.

Around them, teams of nurses and doctors rushed in every direction. This was obviously a big emergency.

In the throng of busy people, Ashley saw three white-coated doctors—two women and a man—clutching clipboards, bounding through the swinging doors behind the paramedics and Mrs. Hudson. She smiled as she watched them go.

Edwina. Ned. And Norma.

"Why are you smiling?" Jason asked, his voice choked with worry.

"Because I know your mother is in good hands," she replied. "The very best hands. Don't worry, Jason. She's going to be just fine."

"See? Things usually turn out for the best," Rachel said. She sat in Ashley's room on her bed a week later, weaving Ashley's hair into a thick French braid.

On the rug, at the end of the bed, Christina sat beside Katie and laid out a pattern of tarot cards. "From the way the cards are falling, it looks to me like you've made a big change in your life, Ashley," she observed. "Inside, I mean."

"I feel like I have," Ashley agreed thoughtfully.

"In what way?" Katie asked, looking up from Madame Rosa's business card, which she'd been examining intently.

"I'm not sure," Ashley admitted. "I feel older somehow. Like I have a better idea of what's important. It's hard to describe."

Molly walked into the room with her cordless phone to her ear. "Great. Oh, that's great. Hang on a minute. Here she is, Jason." She held the phone out to Ashley.

Ashley eagerly took the phone. "Hi. How's your mom feeling today?" Jason told her that his mother was much better. The doctors had told him she was healing well and should make a full recovery.

"She knows she never should have waited so long to get help," he told Ashley. "The doctors are starting her on a new medicine today, and she'll be home tomorrow. They're going to send a visiting nurse to our house every day for the next few weeks to keep an eye on her."

Ashley smiled to herself. Jason sounded so happy. He hadn't stammered once, but Ashley decided not to mention it. Why make him self-conscious?

"I'm so glad for you and your mother," she said sincerely.

"Thank you, Ashley. Thanks for everything. If you hadn't been there, I don't know what I would have done," he said.

"I'm glad I made it," she replied. It was true, too. When she'd been trailing after Dar in Newland, she'd felt so small and meaningless. Helping Jason had given her back her sense of self-worth.

Saying good-bye to Jason, she clicked off the cordless phone and turned back to her friends. "I'm going to invite him to the dance," she said with sudden conviction.

"Good for you," said Molly, taking back her phone and placing it in its pouch. "I think he's cute, and nice. He's much better for you than Dar ever was."

"Will you be free in time for the dance?" Rachel asked as she twisted a green and gold stretchy around the bottom of Ashley's braid. Ashley had been grounded when she admitted to her parents that she had sneaked away for the weekend with Dar. She had accepted her punishment quietly, knowing that it would be coming before she made her confession.

"It'll be my first weekend out from under house arrest," she said happily. "I can't think of a better way to celebrate."

Katie knelt up at the end of the bed and laid down Madame Rosa's card. "Can I borrow your phone?" she asked Molly.

When Molly handed it to her, Katie checked the numbers on the push buttons against Gabe's phone number. "I knew it," she cried. "You should have known he was an angel all along, Ashley."

"How?" Ashley asked.

Katie tapped the card. "The first five digits of his phone number—264-3500—spell 'angel.'"

Ashley lifted the card and examined it. "My gosh, you're right." She looked at her friends, wide-eyed. "Do you think he could have been?"

"Of course he was," Katie replied matter-of-factly. "Isn't it obvious?"

Ashley flopped back on her bed, holding the card over her heart. She felt as if she'd been away on a long journey and was finally home. Home with her friends, with her family, and with herself.

Yet, she'd never been as all alone—as far away—as she'd thought. Gabe had been watching her. Gabe had guided her home.

And perhaps Gabe had even guided her to Jason. Time would tell. She recalled the last thing the angel had said to her. "I'll be seeing you."

She hoped it was true.

In her heart, she knew it was.

23

"Are you nervous?" Rachel asked Ashley as they stood outside the cafeteria door. From inside, the music of Human Dilemma boomed at full volume.

"I'm not sure," Ashley admitted. She hadn't seen or heard from Dar since Newland. How would she feel when she saw him onstage? How would he act toward her? "Yes, I guess I am nervous."

"Well, you look beautiful," Rachel assured her.

In the glass of the trophy case, Ashley looked at her reflection. She wore a new blue-green dress, short and simply cut. Black ankle-strapped shoes gave her an inch of extra height. Her long red curls were bundled loosely on top of her head. A little mascara was her only makeup. She felt pleased by the overall effect. "Thanks. You look great, too."

Rachel did look lovely. Her long, silky black hair tumbled down to her waist over a soft white sweater dress.

Up until that moment, they'd been rushing around

behind the scenes, making sure the food and lighting were just right. Now they were ready to relax a bit and enjoy all their friends. "We'd better go in," Rachel prompted. "We are the chairpersons, after all."

Ashley nodded as an anxious feeling churned in the pit of her stomach. She stepped inside, and her eyes locked on Dar. He sure was handsome. Involved in his singing, he didn't notice her.

Ashley studied him, watching him move. The kids really loved the band. They loved Dar. A lot of them were already dancing.

"Ashley!" She turned to the call and saw Christina, Molly, and Katie standing together. Rachel had joined them, too.

As Ashley approached them, she smiled, suddenly feeling more relaxed. With her friends around her, she felt safer.

"Good dance," said Katie. "The band stinks, but the dance is good."

"Do you really think the band stinks?" Rachel questioned, worried.

Katie tossed back her auburn hair in a gesture of firm confidence. She looked terrific in a one-piece denim jumpsuit. "Of course it does. The lead singer is the pits."

Ashley smiled. Katie was so loyal. Anyone who'd hurt Ashley's feelings would get nowhere with Katie. Everything he did would be wrong. Although it wasn't reasonable, Ashley appreciated it.

"I think they're pretty good," Ashley said.

"Well, you're wrong," Katie insisted stubbornly.

Ashley laughed lightly. "I didn't say they were nice, I just said they were good musicians."

"They *are* good," Christina backed her up. "But I think Dar's gained weight. He looks fat to me."

Dar had definitely not gained weight. He still moved with the grace of a cat. Christina was just joining Katie in finding fault with Dar.

Molly gripped Ashley's wrist in a panicky hold. "Darrin Tyson is coming over. What does he want?"

The large boy looked completely ill at ease in a white dress shirt and black dress pants. "He's not going to ask one of us to dance, is he?" Christina gasped, wide-eyed with horror at the idea.

"Hi, girls," he said awkwardly. "What's happening?"

"Nothing much," Katie replied boldly.

He looked at her and nodded. "Feel like dancing?"

Ashley cringed inside. Katie was sure to blow him off with some incredibly rude comment. She almost felt sorry for him. How could he have been foolish enough to let himself in for this public rejection?

"Okay," Katie agreed neutrally.

Ashley swung around to her, mouth opened in stunned surprise. Katie didn't meet her eyes but walked out to the dance floor beside Darrin.

"I don't believe it," Christina breathed.

"I am completely knocked out," Molly agreed.

"He's kind of cute in a huge football-playing jock way," Rachel offered.

Ashley rolled her eyes. Maybe she should have seen it coming. The way Katie and Darrin always tormented each other was probably a sign of mutual liking. When it came to love and romance, she was learning that people could act pretty strange.

Ashley spent the next hour circulating around, making sure the dance was going well. It was. She and Rachel had done a good job planning everything. In between her many jobs, she chatted with her classmates.

The band took a break, and Ashley tensed all over again. Would Dar try to talk to her? What would she say? What would he?

She was at the refreshment table when he came up alongside her. "Hi," she said, her voice surprisingly small.

He looked startled, as if he hadn't noticed her there at first. "Hi," he replied in a flat, noncommittal voice. He didn't look at her directly but concentrated on the food at the table as though it were completely fascinating.

"The band sounds good," she commented stiffly.

"Thanks." He kept loading food onto his plate, not daring to make eye contact.

She studied his profile. It hadn't changed—still perfect—yet she realized she had changed. Her heart wasn't racing at the sight of him. She wasn't trembling just because they were near each other. Inside, she was calm.

She was over him. She remembered how mean he could be. It spoiled his looks. Sure, he was handsome on the outside, but inside, where it really counted, he was anything but.

The realization made her smile. She really didn't care what he did or didn't say or do.

She wondered for a moment if she should talk to him

about what had happened at Newland. But why? He wasn't important anymore. And he seemed to want nothing more than to escape from her. "I've got to go," Dar said as his eyes darted back to the band. "See ya around." Abruptly, he turned and hurried away. She watched as he brought the plate of food over to a dark-haired girl sitting by the band. The girl looked like she was in high school. She was probably Dar's latest love interest.

And it didn't bother Ashley in the least.

As she watched, she sensed someone come up just behind her. "Jason!" she cried, pleased to see him. "I thought you said you weren't coming. Weren't you moving into your new apartment today?"

In the last weeks, Ashley and Jason had become good friends. Since that day they helicoptered his mother out of the woods, he hadn't stammered even once. Yet, he hadn't asked her to the dance, and she had never worked up the nerve to ask him. She'd almost asked him several times in homeroom, but each time she'd chickened out.

"We finished earlier than I thought," he explained. "We really didn't have much stuff, and Mom wanted me to get out of her way for a while. Now that she's feeling better, she wants to do a million things at once. Besides, I knew how important the dance was to you, so I wanted to be here." The last words tumbled out of Jason's mouth so quickly that Ashley wasn't sure she'd heard them correctly.

"I'm glad you're here," she said, smiling at him. They stood together, looking at the kids who were out on the floor dancing. During the band's break, Rachel had put on a tape. Katie still danced with Darrin. Christina,

Rachel, and Molly danced together in a circle. A slow song came on, and the floor cleared.

"Would you like to dance?" Jason invited her.

"I'd like that," Ashley agreed.

Together they walked out onto the floor. Jason put his arms around her waist, and they moved together to the soft melody of the song.

Ashley was pleasantly surprised at how easily they moved together. She'd never been this close to Jason before, but it didn't feel strange.

To her happy amazement, she realized something about Jason. Dancing with him like this made her heart race as it never had before. Was their friendship changing into something more? Was it becoming . . . love?

As they turned, Ashley caught sight of a familiar figure standing by the refreshment table.

Gabe! She gasped.

He smiled and winked at her.

"Is something wrong?" Jason asked. "You just jumped."

"No," she replied. "Everything's fine." She glanced back over his shoulder, looking for Gabe. He had disappeared. Scanning the cafeteria, she couldn't see him anywhere.

"Do you want to sit down?" Jason asked as the music came to an end.

"I'd rather keep dancing," she said quietly.

He smiled and nodded. "Me too." As the next song started, Ashley gently rested her head on his shoulder. Their relationship was definitely changing. Had she found her first real love? Only time would tell, she guessed. But, just now, it felt absolutely right.

FOREVER ANGELS

by Suzanne Weyn

Everyone needs a special angel . . .

Available wherever you buy books.

VISIT PLANET TROLL

A super-sensational spot on the Internet
at http://www.troll.com

Check out Kids' T-Zone, a really cool place where you can...

- Play games!
- Win prizes!
- Speak your mind in the Gab Lab!
- Find out about the latest and greatest books and authors!
- Shop at BookWorld!
- Order books on-line!

And a UNIVERSE more of GREAT BIG FUN!

To order a free Internet trial with CompuServe's Internet access service, Sprynet, adults may call 1-888-947-2669. (For a limited time only.)